Also by Laurel McHargue

Hai CLASS ku: Classroom Warm-ups

Haikus Can Amuse: 366 Haiku Starters

Hunt for Red Meat (love stories)

"Miss?"

The Hare, Raising Truth

Waterwight Flux: Book II of the Waterwight Series

Waterwight: Book I of the Waterwight Series

Waterwight
Breathe

Book III of the Waterwight Series

Waterwight World Map

Waterwight
Breathe

Book III of the Waterwight Series

Laurel McHargue

STRACK PRESS

STRACK PRESS LLC   Leadville, CO

This is a work of fiction. All characters, places, and events portrayed in this book are the product of the author's imagination. Any resemblance to actual persons, living or dead, events, or locales is entirely coincidental.

Waterwight Breathe
Book III of the Waterwight Series

Published by Strack Press LLC
Leadville, CO

FIRST EDITION 2019

Library of Congress Control Number: 2018901900
McHargue, Laurel, Author
Waterwight Breathe
Laurel McHargue

ISBN: 978-0-9969711-3-3

Edited by Carol Bellhouse and Stephanie Spong
Cover Design by Trif Andrei and Trif Paul, TwinArtDesign

Printed in The United States of America

For

Carol Bellhouse—
who heard the word *Waterwight*,
and whose chapter-by-chapter bubble bath editing
of this final book kept me on track
until the final page . . .

and

Stephanie Spong—
who read my "completed" manuscript
and provided ample evidence to support the fact that
I wasn't even close to being finished yet!

It took we three Muses
to create these three books!

Table of Contents

Waterwight Breathe   1

Acknowledgments   189

About the Author   191

Synonym Glossary   193

Questions for Discussion   201

~ 1 ~

WHY AM I in a black velvet cocoon? It doesn't matter. It's safe in here. Warm and quiet and so, so soft. I'm going to stay here forever. Why would a butterfly ever want to leave such a place?

But I'm not a butterfly. I'm a dove. No! I'm a girl. Oh, who cares? I'm safe and warm and no one will find me here. If they can't find me, they can't kill me, right?

My friends. I think I remember friends. Did I have friends? I saved them when I cured the water, didn't I? But I didn't really cure it after all. Odin held me in his hand and opened the clouds beneath us and . . .

Wait a minute. That can't be right.

No. Must've been a dream. I'm a big dreamer. Mom and Daddy love to hear my dreams when I come down for breakfast in the morning. Crisp bacon and sunshine eggs and toast the color of autumn wheat—Mom has a gift for breakfast—and I'll share my dreams as soon as I wake up today. But not yet. I'm not ready yet.

My head feels fuzzy and light, like it might disappear from my body. Weird. The thought of disappearing makes me feel tingly. Is this how a little larva feels as it melts into goo before rearranging itself into a butterfly? Caterpillar soup. I feel like warm, caterpillar soup.

What kind of butterfly could I be when I emerge? A peacock butterfly comes to mind. Peacocks have the most awesome feathers of all. Monarchs are beautiful too, like stained glass windows.

Mom has lots of art books filled with photos of old churches with huge stained glass windows. Who washes all those colorful panes?

Then there's the Ulysses butterfly with the most striking blue, outlined in black, and it looks like a teardrop falls from each lower wingtip.

Teardrops. When I cried and my tears hit the ocean below, they caused a tsunami around the world. Did that really happen?

The Queen Alexandra's birdwing butterfly has all my favorite colors: green, blue, and yellow. And they're really big, the biggest. Almost a foot wide. About as big as I was when I was a . . .

No. That can't be right either.

The glasswing butterfly is astounding. Lots of butterflies have a stained glass pattern, but my butterfly book says you can see right through this one's wings, like you're looking through a window. So delicate and fragile. They remind me of Orville's wings.

Wait. A flying frog named Orville? I heard him in my dreams. He rescued me when I was falling into the ocean. But I haven't thought about my butterfly book in a long time. Why am I remembering it now?

Oh, right. I'm in a cocoon. And I want to stay here because . . . because . . .

Something's calling me, but I don't want to go. I'd have to open my eyes and rise. I'd have to figure out who, or what, is calling me, and why.

And I'd have to remember. I'd have to remember my friends aren't safe, and Mom and Daddy are gone.

I don't move a muscle, don't open my eyes. It almost works. Something tingles on the back of my head, like I'm melting, but that makes no sense. There's a water-drop mark somewhere back there, or so I'm told. So I remember being told. But that makes no sense either.

Just stay asleep. Sleep is good. Sleep is healing. Sleep is escape.

"Help me," a voice once called me in a dream. "Help *her*," it said.

A giggling girl lured me into a trap. The memory makes my heart race faster than the three hearts in Zoya's battered body. I almost wake up.

But no. Zoya was just a dream. Had to be. A submarine with bad people lodged inside a gigantic octopus? One of my dark dreams. Harmony must've been a dream too.

There was a dog. A dog named Ranger. Ranger knew more about me than I knew about myself. He'd look at me with those honey-brown eyes and I believe he saw things in my future. He always looked so sad.

My face is wet. I feel a tickle on my cheek. Probably Ranger coming in to wake me for breakfast. His little puppy tongue makes me giggle.

The sound of my laughter startles me awake and I open my eyes to darkness. Something drips from above me, wetting my face and running down my cheek like tears. My head throbs and swirling colors flash through my brain. My cocoon has dissolved, but I'm no butterfly.

I'm a frightened girl curled up in the fetal position on a cold slab of stone.

~ 2 ~

I FREEZE when I hear his voice.

"Celeste? Say something, daughter! Tell us where you are! We're here to take you home!"

"Daddy?" The sound of my voice reverberates in the cavernous enclosure, but I must've been dreaming again. I dreamt my father was calling my name, talking about home. I force myself to my feet. My head's fuzzy. His voice sounded so real, but what can I trust anymore? Talking animals, a mountain spirit, a flying frog, battling deities, the octopus . . .

Was any of it even real?

"Nick? Are you there? Chimney? Where are you?" Where are we? I hear the echo of my beating heart and search for my friends. My friends were just with me, weren't they?

"Oooo, ouch! Is anybody there? I'm ascared!"

It's Chimney, crying in the darkness. He sounds real, so I answer. I remember losing my grip on his hand in the violently churning water current. I lost Nick's hand too.

"I'm here, Chim, don't be afraid." Finally I can see—the boulders surrounding us glow a cool green—and holding his stomach, Chimney sits against a slab of cold granite. Before I get to him, he vomits a gush of water.

"Eewww, yuck," he says. His face searches in my direction. He can't see me. "Celeste? Where are you? Where are we? Where's Nick?"

Where's Nick.

I work to reconnect the events leading to this moment. Sleeping, dreaming, everything so fuzzy. Talking. Floating. A kiss . . .

I hear moaning farther back in the cavern, but first I have to comfort a frightened boy. I take his hand, and before I speak, he jumps into my arms and clings to me like a little octopus.

I remember Zoya and the last message I relayed to Harmony. Was she successful in releasing the punished creature from the intruders? Not a dream, then.

"It's me, Chim. Are you okay?" I look him over and determine he's battered, but not too badly. The strength of his embrace tells me what I need to know.

"I dunno. What happened?"

The moaning grows louder.

"Here, hold my hand. Let's find Nick," I say. "A big water current pushed us into this place. Remember?"

"Oh, yeah. I tried to hold on." His hand grips mine as if it's a lifeline.

We stumble and crawl over boulders until I see him.

"Nick! We're here!" I call to him.

Blood drips down his face, but he pushes himself to a standing position before we reach him. No obvious broken bones.

He searches in the darkness for my voice, and I'm grateful for my ability to see in darkness.

"It's me and Chimney. We're in some kind of cave. The current must've carried us here. I thought I'd lost you in it! Here, let me take a look at your head."

The gash over his eye is bad; it'll need to be stitched closed, or Ryder will need to heal him back in the village.

That is, if we can find our way out of this cave and home, and if the boy still has healing powers.

Home.

Nick doesn't focus on me. He holds his hands out in front of him as if protecting himself from me. He looks angry.

"Stay away from me!" He stumbles backward and falls over one of many obstacles, and I rush to him.

"Nick, it's me, Celeste! You're hurt! Please let me help you." I hold his shoulders down to keep him on his back. How am I going to stop his head from bleeding, and why is he acting like this? Didn't he just kiss me a little while ago?

His eyes turn toward my voice and I see panic in them.

"Celeste?" he says.

"Yes! And Chimney's here too."

"Celeste? Chimney? Who are you? What did you do to me? Where am I?"

Nick tries to disengage from my grasp, but I'm stronger than he is—at least for now—and I catch my breath. He doesn't know us.

"Whaddaya mean, who are we?" Chimney moves around to Nick's other side and grabs his hand. "I'm your best buddy, aren't I?" He sounds hurt.

I need to take charge, but I hear someone calling my name again from far away. It sounds like my father, but it can't be him. Not in this place, wherever this place is. Not anyplace, really. He disappeared years ago.

The voice calls me. Nick doesn't remember me. Maybe none of us is who we think we are.

"Nick, you're hurt and I need to find something to bind that gash on your forehead." I peer around the cavern as if there'd be bandages just lying around, and then I spot something hanging out of his pocket.

It's my emerald green scarf, the zigzag blood stain from my own head wound still fused with its fibers.

"You kept my scarf," I say, letting it drape in front of his face.

"Scarf?" he asks, reaching a hand out to feel it.

"Never mind. I'm going to wrap this around your head, and you're just going to have to trust me. Do I look like someone who'd want to hurt you?" My heart squeezes. How could he think I'd ever want to hurt him?

"I don't know. I can't see you."

"But you can hear her, Nick, and you can hear me, right? And we're your friends, and you're gonna be okay, isn't he, Celeste?"

"Yes, Chim." Just handle one crisis at a time. I've grown used to harsh predicaments since The Event shattered our world. What's this but one more? I've gotten used to my life being an endless stream of insane trials.

No, I haven't, really.

I take Chimney's hand and guide his fingers to hold the gash closed. Nick allows me to secure my scarf over it and around his head, and I hope the salty water will help to keep it clean.

"Celeste. You . . . are safe," a familiar voice booms.

"Old Man Massive! Is that you?" It couldn't be anyone else. There's no way I'd mistake his resonant voice. Despite his assurance of safety, I flinch in fear of falling debris as his words rumble the cave walls. Chimney jumps across Nick and clings to me again.

"Yes. It is I. Your father waits for you above."

My head swims and I feel like I might throw up. I've been tricked too many times already. I'm done with being the naïve child I once was. That little girl is gone.

"My father's dead, Old Man." It's the first time I've uttered the words. "I saw him fall." He, my mother, my puppy, they all fell into a stinking, house-ripping fissure the day of The Event. They couldn't have survived it.

"But you are wrong, child. Go to him."

I want to trust the mountain spirit—

"You have a dad? Can he fly too?"

On the heels of Old Man Massive's statement, Chimney's question makes my heart skip a beat. Do I dare to hope?

"No, Chim—"

"Celeste? Are you in there?"

It sounds like the father I remember. My heart flutters again and I want to scream, "I'm here, Daddy! I'm here! Please help!" but I don't. I know it's just another trick. I want to see him so badly I'm afraid to believe. I can't be tricked again. Last time, it nearly killed me.

"I need to get Nick home," I speak to the stone above me. If we're truly inside Old Man Massive, we're a long way from the village and I have no idea what powers I still have, if I have any at all. If I ever even *had* any at all.

I turn my attention to Chimney.

"Here, Chim. You stay on Nick's other side and we'll find a way out, okay?" I place one of Nick's hands on Chimney's shoulder and take his other hand in mine. He feels cold.

"They will help you home," the mountain whispers. He sounds sad.

"They?" I ask, but the answer won't matter.

I'm not sure what matters anymore.

~ 3 ~

NICK AND CHIMNEY MATTER. They're the closest people I have to family. They risked their lives to rescue me. Kumugwe told Harmony that "if their intentions are pure," they'd survive underwater in this new world, but I didn't need for them to suffer through such a distressing experience to convince me of their loyalty.

Nick's kiss. So warm and tentative. It shook me from a waking sleep I couldn't escape from while I was in Kumugwe's castle. Will there ever be a time we'll be together for whatever might remain of forever?

"Never forever," Orville once told me. But that was a lifetime ago.

A lifetime ago I ran away. A lifetime ago I was tricked into believing I was home. A lifetime ago . . .

I was plunked into the ocean to help Harmony free Zoya from unspeakable anguish, and it's slowly becoming clear why. Harmony was just a child. *Was.* But the voice I heard speaking to Kumugwe was the voice of a young woman. Something must have happened to her during the fluxes, but even though she might have changed physically, it doesn't mean she matured mentally or emotionally.

Or can knowledge and maturity be loaded into your brain, given to you like a gift from the gods? Seems anything's possible in this unstable universe. But no. I would have thrown the spear and known where to throw it to stop the abominable metal heart keeping Zoya alive.

I felt Harmony's hesitation as if it were my own and told her what to do. Pretty sure she heard me—felt me, like we were one—and was successful. A fleeting sense of calmness washed over me moments before the water heaved and—

"Whoa! Cool!" Chimney's exclamation shakes me from the swirling turmoil in my brain. He's pointing toward my feet, and when I look down, I see why his eyes are so wide.

With each step I take, a surge of glittering green illuminates the surface we're walking on and spreads upward around us. I can feel them, but I can't actually see my feet. It's like they've dispersed into the stuff of the stones and gravel inside the cave and given life to the cold grit.

"Old Man?" I beckon the mountain spirit, though I question his reality.

"Yes, little Paloma?"

Little Paloma. Little dove. A name from a lifetime ago. It is him. He is real. "Thanks for the light," I say.

"Light, child?"

"This green glow," I say. "It's helpful, the way you're lighting this space for us."

"This is not a thing I can do." He sounds perplexed.

So, it's me. I'm somehow creating light.

"Don't worry!" I call to the mountain spirit. "I figured it out!"

Nick stumbles, and I catch him. "Let's stop a bit. I want to check your head." I encourage Nick to sit while Chimney scoops up and tosses handfuls of illuminated gravel into the air. Nick opens his eyes in an expression of awe as the particles twinkle overhead like stars in a constellation before bouncing back onto the convoluted pathway ahead.

While Nick gazes beyond me, I try to keep my face a blank page. My emerald scarf is more red than green. I try not to panic. I tear off the bottom of my shirt.

"This will help keep my scarf in place," I say with feigned confidence, and he doesn't protest when I tie it snugly over the flimsy scarf around his head. "Now, come on, let's get out of here." He lets me pull him to his feet. He's less combative. Less alert.

"Hey, Old Man," I raise my voice, "how much farther until we're out?"

Ooo. I haven't even asked how he's been since I saw him last. I've been too wrapped up in my own challenges. It's hard to remember others haven't exactly been enjoying an easy life either.

"Hard for me to say," he tells me. "When I collapsed to catch you—"

"What? What do you mean, collapsed?" I try to visualize what it would mean for a mighty mountain to collapse.

"I felt the surge of a great wave," he says.

The story of how he saved our lives unfolds slowly. Sensing the wave, he collapsed the rocky precipice I'd jumped from that first time I left him, and somehow swallowed us into a safe space inside. If he hadn't, we'd have been smashed against the wall.

"But, you're still here! Are you hurt? How did you know we were in the surge?" I sound like Chimney, asking all these questions, and as if he hears his name in my head, my little friend chimes in.

"Yeah, mister, how'd you know?" He searches in the dark for the face belonging to the voice.

"I sense things as they approach. I sensed you, Celeste, the first time we met. Your vibration is distinct; I felt it in the surge. It felt . . . troubled. Stones do not hurt, though. And I remain here, as I have throughout the ages, though you may not be able to see me as easily amidst the rubble."

"You saved us, Old Man. And I've missed your guidance." I wrap my arm more tightly around Nick, whose copper skin has lost its luster. "But, do you know how far we have to go to get to the surface? Nick is hurt, and I have to get him home." I shake off a wave of claustrophobia under the weight of all this stone.

"I brought you far in, away from your pursuers," the mountain spirit tells me.

I glance over my shoulder, though I'm certain we three are the only ones in the cave. "Someone was following us?" I can't imagine who or what. No mere mortal could have navigated purposefully in the turbulent force of the surge.

But a god—

"A girl, who is a fish," he says, "and behind her, the one who rules the waters."

Raised by Kumugwe, Harmony is surely a strong swimmer, but she's not a fish. "Harmony and Kumugwe, the water god," I say. "Did you see them? Or how—"

"I am in the stone you see above and below the water's surface, child. Yes. An alabaster girl with the tail of a fish, and behind her, the monster fish-god."

"Are they okay? Where are they?"

"The girl swims around a small island mountain I formed to stop the monster. Kumugwe is a fish out of water, trapped in a special mountain cave."

"C'mon, Celeste! Look, a hallway!"

I want to ask more questions, but Nick is fading and Chimney is pulling me toward an opening in the walls.

"Celeste? Is it you?"

I hear my name again echoing from a long way off. Could someone, something be pretending to be my father? Has Harmony created an imitation of him on land? She had me fooled in her sandcastle. But now I know her tricks. It won't happen again.

"Follow my voice, Little Bear!"

Little Bear! Would Harmony have known the pet name my father had given me after he taught me about stardust and the constellations? He was Big Bear, Ursa Major, and I was his Little Bear. She couldn't have known this.

My heart leaps, but I don't respond. Not yet. Not until I see him. Not until I can look into his eyes. I'll know then if something's wrong.

I don't need Chimney's help to hold up Nick anymore. I release his hand and follow him toward the opening, conscious of Nick's growing weight upon me as he loses his ability to walk. The walls reflect the glow radiating from my footsteps.

"Looks like Chim's found a way out," I tell Nick, talking to him as if to a child. But his focus remains on the glittering green light swirling up around us. He doesn't respond to my comment.

The hallway twists and turns and rises and falls and sharp stones jut from every angle, so I'm constantly guiding him to prevent another head injury. He stumbles frequently. Will I ever get him out, ever get him home, ever get him back to me?

Old Man Massive saved us from smashing against a rock wall. He can't let us die deep within his rubble. I call to him again.

"You say that's my father calling me. How do you know it isn't a trick?"

The mountain spirit pauses before answering. "This man's vibration. It matches yours, little dove."

I feel like I might burst, so I take a slow, deep breath, and focus on what's most important.

Searching Nick's viridian eyes for a sign of remembrance, I whisper, "Thank you for finding me. How did you know where to look?"

And then I see it. It's just a flicker, but it's there. He returns my gaze, still somewhat puzzled, but searching for something too.

"Celeste!" Our moment is interrupted by the voice of a man who could be my father. And it's close. But I'm encouraged by the flash in Nick's eyes and determined to confront whatever lies ahead.

"Is that your dad, Celeste? Will he take us home?" Chimney points toward an approaching shadow far down the passageway. I see a tiny glimmer of daylight behind the shape, and then, the unthinkable happens.

"Stop!" Nick yells, and everything, including Nick, freezes in time and space.

~ 4 ~

NO. THIS CAN'T BE HAPPENING. But it is.

Nick and Chimney and the shadow at the end of the tunnel are all statues. I catch my breath—what if Nick's power had stopped me too?

He trapped himself this time, though, and I don't know what the consequences will be. I look into his eyes again hoping to see some indication of awareness. Nothing. He just looks surprised. He trapped himself in the nick of time. It's an expression I remember my parents using when they'd catch me right before doing something foolish. "Good thing we stopped you in the nick of time," they'd say.

He's my Nick of time. But how do I get him back?

I need to know what's casting that shadow. I need to know if it's really my father. But what if Nick's hold on time slips while I'm gone? He could hurt himself more. And if the shadow's something bad, it could hurt me.

I have to know. I can't stand the suspense any longer.

"Nick, I know you're in there and you're probably upset, but don't be," I tell him. Maybe he can hear me and just can't move yet. "Please remember who you are, Nick. I know you'll release yourself and Chimney soon, when you're ready." If I'm not here when he's ready, he'll fall. "I'm going to lay you down so you can rest a bit."

His head injury could have strengthened his power. Maybe he knew, subconsciously, he could heal faster if he froze himself.

"They're not really frozen," he told me back in the village forever ago. He explained how he'd just think the word "stop" and everything around him would seem to freeze in time.

I remember Teresa's doves suspended in flight above her as she worked in her garden, and how startled I was when I touched her arm and heard her voice in my head. That was forever ago too.

This time, though, Nick *shouted* the word. Maybe that's the key.

Searching for keys—my life's labor.

"I'm going to check out whatever's down there, so stay here until I come back." It's not like he could go anywhere right now anyway, and I could be wasting my time, but what does time even mean when it's stopped all around you?

I turn to leave, then hesitate. I want to shake him out of his spell. Instead, I kiss his lips softly. Maybe what he did for me will wake him too. But no. It doesn't work.

He's cold, and it scares me. "Come back to me, Nick," I whisper close to his ear. Looking in his eyes again, I see a hint of a change, or maybe I just wish I see it. "I'll be right back and we'll go home."

I check on Chimney and he seems fine, except for the frozen-in-time part. "Hey, Chim, we'll go home soon. You stay here with Nick and I'll be right back." No change in his expression. I'll bet he wishes he could use his own power and disappear.

It's time to face the shadow. But before I leave my friends, I wonder about the reach of Nick's power.

"Old Man? Are you there?" I look up as if the mountain spirit is above us, but that's ridiculous. He's all around us, in every fallen stone and even in the spaces we can't see.

"I am here." His powerful voice comes to me in a strained whisper. "What . . . has happened?"

"Nick stopped time and trapped himself too," I tell him. "Did you feel it?" I can't imagine Nick's power would have any effect on an ancient spirit. That idea scares me too.

"Yes," he confirms my fear. "I feel drowsy."

Old Man Massive has slept for eons. "I don't like this," I tell him. "What if I can't—"

"You will find a way." He cuts me off with words wrapped in a yawn.

"I'm going to see who's at the end of the tunnel," I tell him, and wait for him to advise me. But nothing. "Old Man?" Nothing. "Old Man Massive," I say more forcefully. Nothing. He's asleep. I hope.

The shadow remains motionless. I'm torn between running to the man casting it—wanting to get it over with quickly—and taking my time, hoping Nick's spell will release while I still have time to react.

While I still have time. I've never *had* time. Time is an idea like home, and I don't have that either. I shake off a shudder when memories of that horrific day flash through my brain.

A rumbling from the very center of the planet, windows rattling, dishes and artwork crashing to the floor, my puppy whimpering under a table, my parents' eyes growing wider as they reach for me, as the floor splits between us, as they call to me with their arms outstretched, as they fall into a fissure between us—reaching for me—calling my name—my childish voice calling theirs—Mommy! Daddy!—they're gone into the void, the reeking void! And I am left alone, unconscious, in the rubble.

Will the smell of sulfur ever leave my nostrils? Will the sound of their screams—and mine—ever stop echoing in my ears?

No.

I run toward the shadow until I'm almost there, and skid to a stop the moment the man's features emerge. He looks like my father. Older than I remember, but that makes sense. There's gray in the hair around his ears and in the cowlick on his forehead. The cowlick—just like mine! I remember how he'd cuss in the morning trying to comb it flat like the rest of his hair.

But it can't be him. It can't. Even if Old Man Massive says otherwise.

"Don't believe it, it's a trick," I say aloud in an attempt to convince myself. But he looks more real than the fake father Harmony conjured when she had me trapped in her sandcastle. I don't remember the fake one having a cowlick.

I tiptoe toward him and close the gap between us silently, afraid to wake him, afraid he'll call me daughter and I'll allow myself to be wrapped in his protective arms, afraid that once I'm safe in his arms . . . I'll die.

I touch his outstretched hand. It feels real, and warm. I touch the stubble on his cheeks and chin. I look into his eyes and see—

"Daddy?" I look for a response, expecting none, seeing none. "Dad?" I try again anyway. I'm a big girl now. Shouldn't be calling him daddy.

It's him. There's no way Harmony could have known about the tiny green dots in the blue irises of his eyes or the freckle hidden in his right eyebrow, difficult to distinguish with his skin the color of copper too, but I can see it.

My throat constricts and tears spill. My insides ache and I allow myself to sob, sinking to the dusty ground, crying until I can laugh at the blob of mud my tears have created.

I wipe my eyes and stand.

My father is alive! That means my mom could be alive too! We can be a family again, and we can live in the village with the others who've lost their parents—or we could rebuild on this side, where our home used to be!

But now what do I do? Am I the only one free of Nick's hold?

Beams of light from the opening beyond beckon me. My sides ache from minutes or hours of crying. I'm in no hurry to discover what's out there, though. I've just found my father—if only he'd shake himself from this spell! And what's hurrying but a desire to speed time, or maybe even to slow it down?

Time isn't real anymore. It never was.

I have to see what's out there, though, so I'm ready for it, but first I look into my father's eyes again hoping to see them respond.

"Dad? I'm here. Your Little Bear's here." There's no change, so I stifle another sob and wrap my arms around him gently and wait to feel him hug me back. He can't, though, and the waiting is agony.

Finally, I let go and walk toward the opening, slowing as the light increases, squinting until my eyes adjust. I don't want to walk into another trap. My heart races as I get closer to whatever waits for us.

"Old Man?" I whisper this time, hoping he might be there for me. Hoping he'll tell me to remember who I am. But he doesn't. I have to remember on my own.

I'm Celeste Araia Nolan. I'm more than just a girl. I've done things.

Out I go.

The air smells clean and cool and I'm in the middle of a slow, deep breath when I see him. A handsome, copper-colored man with wings is stopped in mid-stride toward me. I approach him as I approached my father—my father!—and feel a curious connection to the stranger.

I touch his radiant emerald wings, but pull my hand back quickly. He is helpless. I'm the aggressor. "Sorry," I say. My parents taught me better than this. And then I look into the man's eyes. His jade green eyes, flecked with gold. It can't be him. Can it?

Holy moly, it is!

"Orville?"

~ 5 ~

"ORVILLE! IT'S YOU!" Why should I be surprised he's a man? An emerald-winged man. The last time I saw him, he was a wind-up metal frog, carrying the shapeshifting vulture out to sea, sacrificing himself for the rest of us. I remember the weight of the wind-up key in my pocket after he flew away.

Nothing should surprise me anymore, but it does. Orville doesn't respond.

I glance around quickly. Can't let my guard down in a world still in flux. Everything is silent, too silent, probably because of Nick's last command.

Nick did it to protect me. It's a nice thought, but since he doesn't recognize me, I shake my head. Surrounded by people I love and who love me, I feel more alone than ever.

How did Dad find Orville? Or did Orville find him? And for how long will Nick's power stop time on this side of the big water?

This side was once my home. I remember feeling safe in my house with Mom and Dad. I didn't know the meaning of responsibility then, or what it meant to feel burdened.

I gaze around at the rubble surrounding the entrance to Old Man Massive's cave, and then out across the cracked, dried fields toward the farm where I had my first standoff with Ranger and his wild pack and where I first met Sharon, toward the children's home that once kept me safe—but safe like a captive is safe.

I gaze toward home.

And then it occurs to me. If Dad is here—it hardly seems possible, but he's here—then why not our house, with Mom in the kitchen smelling of honey-lemon muffins and making eggs and bacon, and my fat puppy romping around her feet? It's possible. The fluxes could have reversed the chaos they created.

And if she's there, I'll fly her back to where Dad and my friends are and we'll be together when time starts again.

"Orville? If you can hear me, please give me a sign. Anything." I stare again into his kind eyes and wait. And wait. It's excruciating. I can't stand it any longer. "I'm going to find my mother," I tell him. "If you're released before I return, Nick and Chimney are inside the cave. Nick's hurt and doesn't remember me. I'll be right back." I hope he hears me.

I run away from the rubble that was once a majestic mountain. I leap and dare to trust I can still fly, and I do. From high above the silent scene below, I can barely make out Old Man Massive's crumbled features. I wish he would call to me, but enough wishing.

I fly north across the plains, faster and faster. I'm past the old farm when something red catches my eye.

Apples! Apples of every size dot the only tree that stood on the children's home playground. I drop to it and pluck one from its top branches, sink my teeth into its crisp flesh, and slurp its sweetness. I want to fill my shirt with them, but there's nothing to tuck in since I tore off the bottom to tie around Nick's head. I fit several small ones into my pants pockets and shove the apple core with its seeds into a small pocket on my shirt.

I leave to find my home and my mom and bring her to the others, but—

All I see, for as far as I can see once I'm high enough, are ruins amid patches of new growth. Colors of springtime here and there are the only signs of hope for miles and miles and miles. Fissures that opened to swallow and crumble manmade structures years ago have closed and heaved great sections of land, and the water that drowned what was left receded, leaving everything caked in cracking mud.

There will be no sweet-smelling mother waiting for me here.

Celeste? Are you there, ma petite?

Orville's voice in my head startles me from my delusion. "Yes! Yes! I'm here!" I scream too loudly, though there's no one around to hear. "I'm coming back! Did you find the boys?"

I cannot move. I do not know what has happened.

"Don't worry. I'll be there in a jiffy," I tell him. *In a jiffy*. Another funny expression my parents would use. Orville probably never used that expression where he came from, but I'm sure he gets my meaning.

And if he can communicate with me, Nick's spell must be wearing off.

The speed of my return is breathtaking, and in a moment, I land lightly in front of him and his eyes meet mine. I can't help myself, and I throw my arms around him. But he can't reciprocate. He can't move or speak yet, but it shouldn't be long before he's able to. "Sorry! I'm sorry!" I stammer, stepping back fast.

Sorry for welcoming an old friend back from the dead? No, child. Never be sorry for that.

"If I can hear you in my mind, the others should be able to hear me when I talk to them!" My excitement over this realization makes his eyes smile. "My father's alive! But you already know that!" And soon he'll hug me like he did when I was a child. "He's inside with Nick and Chim. Be right back!"

I run to my father, who's still motionless, and his eyes light up when he sees me. I throw my arms around him again, this time not quite as gently.

"Daddy! It's me! I'm safe! And I'll be right back. Nick and Chimney are farther in. They'll be scared." I feel like I'm five again. Or ten. He'll have to wait for an explanation. How I hate to make him wait.

I hurry toward my friends, careful of my footing on the uneven surface as the passage darkens. My eyes adjust quickly, and I notice swirls of emerald glow that seem to surge in unison with the adrenaline I feel pumping through my body.

"Celeste?"

Chimney can speak! That means they'll all be released and we'll be out of the cave in no time, as long as we can keep Nick from using his power again.

"Coming, Chim!" I call to him. I see him turning in a slow circle, looking all around. He'll be irked at Nick for stopping time. I remember him telling Nick "no more funny business" the last time Nick trapped him in time.

He sees me, or probably he sees the green glow from my feet—my feet have disappeared again into the light they radiate—and before I can say another word, Chimney closes the distance between us and just about knocks me over with his greeting.

I hug him, my quirky little buddy who introduced me to snoodles and brought me to his village, and I look over his shoulder, hoping with all my heart that Nick has recovered his senses and will recognize me.

"Chim?" I hold the boy's shoulders and search his eyes. "Where's Nick?"

~ 6 ~

"I DUNNO. I just got unstuck." Chimney squints into the darkness behind him. "I wish he wouldn't do that no more when I'm around. Feels like I'm totally disappeared. It scares me."

"We'll talk to him about it when we see him, okay?" I hug him again. A mixture of excitement, fear, and sadness contorts his innocent face.

"Things are still weird, aren't they? And what if the ooze comes back? Could we breathe in it? Could we really breathe in water when we found you? How? How could we breathe underwater, and why are we here in this cave, and—"

"Celeste? I'm here, Celeste!" My father's voice pulls me away from Chimney's questions—I can't believe Dad's alive, and here—but where's Nick? Do I call out his name? Or would he yell "stop" again? Can't let that happen.

"My father's calling me, Chim. Go to him and tell him I have to find Nick, okay? He'll understand. He's a good guy." I turn to head back into the cave, but stop. "Oh, and Orville's outside too, but he's a man now."

"Yeah, I know," he says, as if I've just told him water's not always blue. "Find him quick, okay? I wanna go home."

He ambles toward my father and I sense his hesitation to leave me.

"I will. He can't be far." *Please-oh-please let this be true.* "I won't be long. Go say hello!" My father is already walking down the passageway toward Chimney. I have to be quick.

Nick must have released himself before his hold wore off of the others, but he could barely walk without my help. He can't be far. Old Man Massive probably knows where he is, but I don't want to ask him. His whispers rumble the surroundings and I don't want to startle Nick again.

It seems I've gone too far when I turn a corner and duck under an obstruction, but there it is—Nick's foot. I approach cautiously. He's slumped against a boulder, eyes closed, breathing so, so slowly. I don't want to wake him . . . and I don't want him to die.

In my softest whisper I say his name. His eyelids flutter and he opens them against an unseen force threatening to hold them closed.

"Pipsqueak," he says, and I can't hold back my tears. "I found you." His eyes close again and his head slumps onto his chest.

No, no, no, no, NO! "Nick, wake up. We're going home."

The space he's crawled into is cramped, but I kneel and wrap my arms around him. His head rests on my shoulder and I feel his heart—still beating!—against mine. I summon the strength of Paloma, the girl inside me with the power to pull jaguars from fissures and turn lake water into raindrops.

He's taller and heavier than I am, but once I get him to a place I can stand, I lift him in both arms and hasten along the passageway. Before I reach the light near the exit, I'm met by my father, Chimney, and Orville—who takes Nick from my arms. My father's eyebrows arch as he studies me for a moment. The reflection of green glow from my footsteps shines in his eyes and he opens his arms to me.

"Daddy!" I'm a child again, choking on my tears with my head buried in his embrace. I don't care about making a fool of myself. I don't care the others might find this moment awkward. I only care that my father is alive and here and I don't have to be the grown-up anymore.

"It's all right, Little Bear," he whispers, swaying softly with my sobs. And then Chimney squeaks, breaking through the heaviness.

"Hey, Celeste? People said your dad was loose in the noodle when he came to our village, but I always knew his crazy words were special and Orville did too."

I lift my head from my father's chest and shake off a moment of embarrassment. They're all looking at me with concern in their eyes and I see Nick, a ragdoll in Orville's arms.

Chimney's words sink in.

"You've been to the village?" I ask my father.

"Yes, though I'll admit I wasn't in my right mind for quite some time."

There it is again. Time. Quite some time.

"But we'll have time to catch up once we get back and care for your friend there." He nods toward Nick.

Will we?

"Mason—ah, your father—is right," Orville tells me, and I notice his troubled expression.

"Can we get outta here?" Chimney digs his toe into a patch of gravel and looks toward the light outside. "And how're we gonna get home?"

It's the question troubling Orville. I see it in his eyes. Sure, he has wings, but how powerful are they? Are they powerful enough to carry an unconscious boy and another across an expansive body of water? And I can fly, but for how long, how far, before another flux might occur?

"Let's go." Dad takes my hand and Chimney's and leads us out of the cave. Orville follows, and when I look over my shoulder I notice how carefully he carries Nick.

When we're just outside the mountain, Old Man Massive speaks. "The dragonfly may return for you, but you must summon her, little Paloma."

"She carried us here," my father says, his eyes filled with optimism.

"Her name is Noor." Orville looks at me expectantly.

"But she dropped me into the water!" I tell them. "I could have drowned!" I feel panicky and jittery and I want to run away. The thought of calling her makes no sense to me until I remember I didn't drown, and she also saved me from Odin's pursuing ravens. I march around the group in a small circle, watching as my feet kick up dust, trying to make sense of nonsense.

"She said I had more to learn, and I had to find and release her—the octopus." I narrate the events as I remember them, not as an explanation to my father and friends, but as a way to trigger an idea that might help me do what I need to do.

And I have to figure it out fast, before life runs out of the boy who makes me feel alive.

"Maybe you have to find her in the sky, Celeste," Chimney offers. "You can see way far away when you're up in the sky, right?"

"My daughter flies," I hear my father whisper.

I look to Orville, who nods, and decide it's worth a try. But first, I call her name.

"Noor!" I shout to the sky, and the others join me. We call and call, but our voices sound puny in the vast open space, and I can't wait any longer. "I'll find her!" I yell before lifting into flight. I'm far, far above them when it happens. The mark on the back of my head begins to tingle.

~ 7 ~

I HEAR HARMONY. Tingling gives way to something else, something familiar, and I hear her weeping.

I stretch impossibly thin—no, never again think *impossible*—dissolving into molecules in the atmosphere, and her voice resonates in me. I know it's her because even though she weeps, there's a lilting, childlike melody surrounding each sob. It makes me want to cry with her.

If only I could trust her, now that I've connected with her in some strange way, but I can't get distracted. I'm up here to summon a fire-breathing dragonfly to help us return to the village.

Stretching, dissolving, it feels good, like a sun sneeze or an unabashed yawn. I've done this before in the water, slipping through the strands of seaweed in an underwater castle, escaping from the room in which the fish god held me prisoner, wanting with all my heart to return to an exhausted, beautiful octopus to stop her three hearts from their cruel, unnatural beating.

I was frightened then, afraid of being destroyed by the returning god's surge toward me through the water, and in snapping back to my body, I was trapped and imprisoned once more.

In my body, I'm vulnerable. But what am I, if not a body expanded? A featureless body, but still somehow me.

Funny. I don't question how I can hear things, see things, feel things in my new me, my unencumbered me.

She cries. She's searching for the only father she knows, swimming around the island in which he's trapped—trapped like he locked his brother in his sea-filled castle room, and like he imprisoned me.

The dry island cavern has rendered Kumugwe ineffective—I feel this too—but like his brother god, Odin, he won't die. One's strength is diminished out of water, the other's, in it.

Maybe a taste of their own medicine will show them that powers like theirs, god-powers, shouldn't be wielded carelessly. Maybe the gods can be made to learn what it's like to be human.

To be vulnerable.

And so I'll let Kumugwe's sea child weep for him, swimming around the little island as a beautiful alabaster mermaid—I see this too—knowing they'll be together again when the time is right.

When the time is right. There's been nothing right about time for as long as I can recall.

Yes, she will swim around the island and—wait! She knows I'm here far above her! She treads water with her glimmering tail and strains her eyes to the heavens. She's searching for me, though in my dispersed state I know she won't see me.

"He'll be okay," I tell her in a way I haven't done before. It's as if a piece of me has detached and is inside her, a part of her, but not even that. More like I *am* her, and I'm still me too. It's magical. It's startling. It's . . . god-like.

It's frightening.

She knows I'm in her, talking to her, and she doesn't know how to respond.

"Celeste! You're alive!" She says these words aloud, looking all around her as if she'll see me soon. "And the others? Your friends?"

The others. My friends. I'm supposed to be looking for Noor.

I detach from Harmony. She'll have to be patient. I need to return my friends to a place called home—unless they, we, are already there. We could definitely rebuild on this side. My father knows construction. We won't have to fly across the water again. We can—

"They'll be completed soon." Another familiar voice distracts me. It's Blanche, but where is she? Still with the scientists? I'll never understand how she was able to abandon Chimney, her only brother.

It seems I've stretched far enough to sense things on the other side, but Noor is nowhere in sight. Bits and pieces of voices and images hit me like I've just stepped under a waterfall and every piece of me vibrates. Blanche is still talking.

"Good thing we got our lab back. The kiddiwinks should be functional—"

What are kiddiwinks? They can't be good things if she and the scientists are involved. *Focus, Celeste.*

Noor! My particles vibrate with her name as I try to block out the other voices, but I might as well be in the lab with them.

"It's not your lab, Blanche, it's theirs. And mine." Another voice breaks through. "I just brought you along to help, you know. You'll do whatever my parents tell you to do."

It's Sharon! She sounds even younger than she did when she appeared at the foot of my bed in the farmhouse. But then she cackles an old lady cackle and every particle of my being shudders. I sense chaos and hostility, a man whimpers, and a woman's voice—harsher than any I've heard before—forces me to pay attention.

"Then, what are you waiting for, girls? Finish your work and get them prepared. There's no time to waste," the woman says, cackling again.

How horrible Sharon's life must have been under that woman's roof.

My thoughts of staying and rebuilding on this side vanish. We have to warn the villagers the scientists are still alive and up to no good.

But how do I find the fire-breathing dragonfly who appeared out of nowhere, or somewhere, scorching Odin's ravens' wings? I feel like I should be able to sense her in my transformed state in the atmosphere, but I've already summoned her like this, to no avail.

I'd need to gather my pieces into my physical body, my girl body, if I want to use Celeste's voice. But it didn't work when I was on the ground with the others. We all called her name, but Noor didn't hear us.

Or she did, and chose to stay away.

I try to concentrate, but I can't remember what I did to return to my human body when I was dispersed in the water. Fear snapped me back then. An intense, abrupt fear.

I focus on tightening all my muscles, but they're hard to imagine in my current diaphanous state. Despite some mental confusion, though, I could get used to this physical form. It makes me feel like I could go and go and go, expanding my yawn until—

"Help me, Pipsqueak."

Until he calls me back.

~ 8 ~

AN INTENSE RUSH snaps me back into my body when I hear Nick's voice, and I'm nearly paralyzed by fear when I see my feet dangling below me in the vast expanse of space. I'll never get used to being able to fly. Fortunately, I can breathe this far up in the atmosphere. I've done it before. I've lived in a realm even more distant from the planet below.

I twirl, leery of Odin's great ravens, but like Noor, they're nowhere to be seen. With Odin trapped in Kumugwe's crumbled castle below, what will they do? What will his wolves do? I can't worry about them. It's Noor I need to find.

I close my eyes and summon her to me in something like a prayer. I did what she asked me to do. I guided Harmony to release Zoya from her agony. I learned things. I stood up to not one god but two, thwarting their attempts to keep me in their realms. What would keep her from coming to me?

But I've waited too long—I can't stay in the heavens. Much like my escape from Asgard, I dart toward the planet where my friends wait. The speed of my flight thrills me— I've never flown so fast—and I laugh aloud until I remember why I'm speeding.

He's calling for my help, but his voice is trapped in his mind. Even though I'm back in my human body, I hear him.

"Noor! Where are you?" Approaching the group below, I try calling her name aloud again, expecting her at any moment to swoop alongside me, but—

"Hurry, Celeste!" It's Chimney. He's jumping up and down, scrunching his shoulders and squeaking. So much agitation for such a young boy. It's not fair.

I land. Nick is ashen in Orville's arms. Without thinking, I take him from my winged friend. There's no time to wait, they know it too. I open my mouth to apologize but my father cuts me off before I can say anything.

"GO!" he shouts, and I'm off on a flight I've taken far too many lifetimes ago, though never at this astounding speed.

Nick feels light in my arms and I fear he's leaving me, leaving his body.

"We're going home," I whisper close to his ear. Wind whistles past us and everything is a visual blur. The space around us warps and the village comes into focus before I lift my lips from his face.

My feet skid a distance on the village road—I've never made such a hasty landing—and a cloud of dust swirls around us.

"Ryder!" I call the name of the boy with healing powers, and before the dust settles, he's running toward us. The whole village is running toward us, as if they've been expecting us. I sit where I am and cradle Nick in my arms. "Help him! Please help him!"

And then I sob.

~ 9 ~

RYDER'S EYES BETRAY HIM. He's afraid. He stares at me as if he's seeing a ghost, but the look on my tear-stained face directs his attention back to his friend, who lies limp in my arms.

I feel like he's afraid for more than Nick, though.

I pull myself together. "You can make him better," I say. "I stopped the bleeding, he hasn't lost too much blood, but he froze time with this head injury and trapped himself too." I don't know how this will help Ryder, but I can't seem to stop talking. "I can hear him in my mind, so I know he's in there. Bring him back, Ryder. Please bring him back."

The crowd mumbles softly around us and I hear my name mentioned. They're all startled to see me. I have no idea how long I've been gone, but the children appear to have grown. The twins, Katie and Lena, rest their hands on my shoulders. They're a little taller, their childlike innocence faded. Have I been away that long? Does a moment spent in the realms of gods stretch into days or months on the planet?

Ryder removes my makeshift bandage, drapes my stained emerald scarf across Nick's chest, lifts Nick's eyelids, and stares into his fading eyes. I stare too, and then something startling happens. I'm looking through Ryder's eyes! He realizes it at the same moment, and his gaze shifts to me.

"What—"

"I don't know," I tell him. "Go back in." I nod toward Nick, and Ryder turns his attention back to his task.

I see what Ryder is seeing. Nick's brain is swollen and pressing against his skull. I feel a pressure in my own head, and I know Ryder feels it too. He probably felt it first. It doesn't really matter. Ryder knows how it should be, and he'll make it right. We'll make it right.

I'm dizzy. I'm in Ryder's head and Nick's head at the same time and it's confusing. I feel Ryder working to visualize space between my—I mean Nick's—brain and skull. He says, "Too much water."

Will there ever be a time we'll feel a balance between too much and not enough water on this planet?

Too much water in Nick's brain is a dangerous condition. I'm in his head and everything's distorted by colorful rivulets of blue and red. I taste the blue copper and the red iron and feel a sudden intense thirst.

"Quickly!" someone shouts. It sounds like Nick, or Ryder—I can't distinguish the voices. I become like a sponge, my particles absorbing excess liquid.

I can't feel how much of me is in Nick's brain—I still feel the weight of him in my lap—so I can't be totally dissolved in him. Part of me wants to stay here, but that can't work.

Slowly, my vision clears. I see Ryder staring intently into my eyes, a slow expression of relief washes over him, and then I see—wait a minute. Then I see me. I'm looking at myself through . . .

It must be through Nick's eyes.

And I don't look so good. I look bloated and scared and there are dark circles under my eyes and my hair is a disaster and what are those purple droplets dripping from my lids? Purple tears?

The murmuring around me grows louder, excitement electrifies voices, and with one stunning snap I'm back in my own head. I look down into the eyes of the boy I hold in my arms and he looks up at me, an exhausted smile hinting at the corners of his eyes and lips. I want to kiss him, but not here. Not now. And looking the way I know I look, I can't imagine he'll ever want to kiss me again.

"Welcome back, Nick." Ryder's voice is sincere, but he still has that frightened expression I noticed before. Nick will be fine, I know this in a place deeper than my bone marrow, so I'll have to ask what's up as soon as we get him some food and rest.

"Thanks, Ryder," Nick says before turning back to me. "I've been dying to see you again, Pipsqueak. Like, seriously dying."

I laugh and cry at the same time, and someone pats me on the shoulder.

"But where's Chimney?" Katie sounds worried.

"And Mason," her sister Lena adds, "and Orville?"

Several others in the group crowd in to hear my answer, and I feel awkward with Nick sprawled across my lap. He's too weak to sit up by himself, so I maintain my grip around him. Awkward or not, he grasps me around the waist and appears to be in no rush to leave me.

"They're on the other side," I say, "and they're safe. I'll find a way to get them back."

Nick squeezes me gently to steal back my attention. "I remember how I woke you up just a little while ago." He whispers this so softly I can barely hear him, and my cheeks feel hot.

He's bolder than I remember. I like it.

"And I have this strange feeling you tried to take advantage of my immobile condition in that cave." His eyes are filled with mischief.

Teresa pretends not to have heard him. "And where have you been all this time, Celeste? We thought we'd never see you again after you threw the spear and disappeared." She lifts a corner of my scarf to wipe the colorful tears from my eyes. Her vision, hearing, and speech are restored. She kneels by my side and lays a hand on my arm, much like I did the first time I met her in her garden. I glance over to the garden and smile at the abundance I see. Her eyes search mine. She's worried about me.

"It's a really long story and I promise to share it with you all, but Nick? How are you feeling?" There's no way I'm going to sit here in the dirt and explain my escapes from the realms of two quarreling gods to a group of people breathing down my neck.

"A little dizzy and really hungry and—" He squeezes me again just a little bit tighter and locks his eyes on mine. "Thank you. Thank you for bringing me home." He looks to Ryder. "And Ryder, thanks again for fixing my noggin."

Ryder lowers his eyes. He looks embarrassed. I can tell he's pleased with the healing he's just managed, but why does he still look frightened? I take a moment to glance around the group and I see the same expression on several faces—relief over Nick's healing, but mixed with fear.

"Here, let me help you." Mac steps from behind Teresa and lifts Nick from my lap. My legs have fallen asleep. I struggle to my feet and feel my muscles wobble.

When the crowd parts to let Mac assist Nick into his house, I hear him—my friend from the other side. He whimpers softly and I see he's been waiting impatiently on the outskirts of the crowd.

"Ranger!" I crouch back down and open my arms, and he winds his way through the dispersing crowd until he's within reach. I throw my arms around him and he gives me a tiny lick under my chin. I'm so happy to feel his full, furry neck. My feet and legs tingle as blood flows back into them. I want to ask him everything, but first things first.

"We'll catch up soon, my friend, but tell me. Why are people afraid? I'll bring back Chimney and Orville and my father—can you believe my father's alive?—but there's something else. What is it?"

"It is the boy, Bridger. He is gone. Taken many nights ago. He would not leave on his own."

"Taken? Who would take him? Why?" As soon as I ask the questions, though, I know who, and I know why. I remember the voices I heard when I was spread across the atmosphere searching for Noor. They took him to rebuild their lab. "Never mind. No need to answer. I'll bring back the others and then we'll find him. Oh, Ranger! It's so good to see you again."

"And you, Celeste. Much has happened since the water cleared." A dog I've never seen before slinks up tentatively behind Ranger and waits.

And then the sky overhead darkens swiftly.

~ 10 ~

IT'S NOOR. She blocks the sunlight and her rapidly beating wings produce a pleasant hum. I hadn't noticed it before; it's soothing. A sense of tranquility replaces the tension-filled atmosphere. She looks down at me with eyes like stars exploding, and the breeze from her wings is surprisingly gentle.

"Why did you abandon us?" I call to her. I'm angry. In our time of great need, she stayed away.

She holds my gaze and I'm lost in the swirling galaxies I see among the shattered stars, but I have my answer.

I had to do it myself. I had to rely on my own speed and strength to save Nick.

Noor doesn't land, her wings would hit the rooftops—*where does she live?*—and I wait for what she might say, for what she might tell me I need to do next.

She says nothing.

Chimney's squeaky voice cuts through the melodic hum of wings. "Here we come, Celeste! Hey, everyone!"

I watch as Orville descends from Noor's back with one arm around Chimney and another around my father. His emerald wings, startlingly large, shimmer as they carry him and his companions back to the ground.

The villagers stand wide-eyed and hushed as Noor disappears into the sky, leaving behind a whoosh of warm wind and silence. A little piece of me wants to follow her, and as I stand, my feet tingle more than they did when my blood flowed back into them. I look to see if they're visible, afraid for a moment they may have dissolved. They look like my feet, though the dust around them glows an emerald green.

The mark on the back of my head tingles too.

"You are changed," Ranger says. He sniffs the dust hesitantly.

"I know," I say, because he's right. And I'm not the only one who's changed. It seems the villagers are no longer divided. The dynamics have changed.

It feels good.

Chimney has my father by the hand and pulls him toward me, and I watch as a beautiful woman runs to Orville's open arms, his wings reflecting the sun brilliantly. She takes him by the hand and leads him off. He belongs to her now, I can sense it, and I feel a little sad—as if I've lost something—but I'm happy for him.

What else has changed since my time with the gods, and what other newcomers have joined the village?

I run to Dad and he lifts me into his arms the same way he used to day after day, years ago. He's real, and somehow we're reunited. It still feels like a dream.

"Let me look at you, daughter!" He sets me back on my feet and, with his hands on my shoulders, stares into my eyes. "I knew you had to be alive. I just knew it. And when I walked from that world beneath the water, I knew someday I'd find you."

I feel a pang for my missing mother, and I can tell he sees it in my eyes. "Dad? Is it possible she—"

Dad shakes his head before I finish my question. "Before I lost consciousness, I saw . . . no. She didn't make it." He pulls me into an embrace again, and we mourn, silently, together.

I notice the villagers moving a respectful distance away to give us a private moment together, and at the same time, I feel their desire to be a part of our reunion—the kind of reunion many of them probably still imagine in their dreams.

After several somber moments, Dad asks, "How's Nick?"

"Resting," I say. "It was close, but Ryder healed him." I don't tell him about how pieces of me dissolved and helped with the repair in his brain. And I don't need to tell him how much I've longed to breathe in the sweet scent of my mother again. He knows. But with his return to me after I'd finally accepted I'd lost them both, I dared to hope for more.

"I wish I could tell you why I survived, Little Bear." Dad chuckles at the nickname. "Look how big you've grown! Your mother would be so proud of you." He holds my face between his hands. "And you have her eyes."

This makes me smile. She's a part of me. "I've missed you both for so long. Where were you, Dad? How did you end up here?"

"All I remember are bits and flashes of visions and feelings. Falling. The vile odor. Fear. Water and motion and a long, long, dream-filled sleep. Then, some kind of water slide and I was walking out of the water with other beings, and the people were all this same color."

The hermit crabs brought him here.

"And what did Chimney mean when he said everyone thought you were, ah—"

"Loose in the noodle?"

"Yes." We both chuckle. It was time to break the sadness.

"I suppose I had what you might call an emotional breakdown. My brain was trying to make sense of everything, but it just couldn't." He looks at me with an intensity I've never seen before. "And I kept feeling like you were out there somewhere, if only I could find you. There were visions. I could see you." He pulls me into a bear hug again and our tears—years of them pent up and repressed—drench his shirt.

"There's so much I need to tell you, Dad." I pull away after the sobbing stops and scratch the back of my head to relieve the tingling. A familiar wave of fear flashes through me when I let go of him—a memory of my time trapped in the sandcastle

"No need to tell me everything now, Celeste. And perhaps we should discuss what happened to Bridger. From what I've witnessed during my short time in the village, he's a powerful little boy."

I hug him tightly once more and call to Ranger.

"Could you track him, Ranger? He's with Sharon's parents. They're treacherous." I recall a hideous vision from when my brain was linked with Harmony's. "They're creating an army of dangerous creatures, and Blanche is with them too. She knew about Bridger's power to build things, so they're probably making him help them somehow."

"I could track him. Yes." Ranger turns to the timid dog behind him and nudges her toward me. "Penelope came to us with evildoers. Ryder healed her after the battle. She knows of places beyond."

Penelope is hesitant to speak to me, but with another gentle nudge from Ranger, she relents. "Outlands are vast. Countless places to hide. I know of some. Not all." She looks to Ranger for assurance, and he moves closer to her. Their sides touch. He's found someone too.

"These evildoers," I say, "are there more?" I envision Sharon's parents gathering together an army of the living to complement their dreadful creatures and I shudder.

"Yes." Penelope's voice quavers, and when I reach out to her, she allows me to touch her. Her trembling stops, and Ranger licks my hand.

"If they need his power, they won't hurt him," I say, as much to convince myself as the others. "He must be scared, though. Let's talk with Orville about the best way to get him back."

"Orville's with Riku. And hey! Where's Nick?" Chimney scrunches his shoulders and looks concerned. "You said he's better, right?"

"Yes! Yes, he's better. I'm sure he's still resting." I feel a sudden urge to be with Nick.

As if sensing my need, Dad nudges me toward the house, keeping a protective hand on Chimney's shoulder. "Go see how he's doing," he says. "I'll stay with Ranger and some of the others and we'll discuss the boy. We'll find him, Celeste."

Dad has probably heard the story of how Nick and Chimney set out to find me. Now it's my turn to hear it. I run to the house and up the stairs to a room I remember he once shared with Mac. The door is closed, and I feel all jittery inside. I don't know what to expect, and I wish I'd stopped to bathe first, but it's too late. I've already cracked the door open an inch.

"Is that you, Pipsqueak?"

I enter tentatively, not sure if I should close the door behind me or open it wider. Why do my legs feel so weak? I close the door.

"What took you so long?" Nick sits up in bed, shirtless, and looks at me expectantly.

What he's expecting, I don't know. He was nearly dead just moments earlier, but now he looks like he did when I first met him. He looks . . . extraordinary. His copper skin glows and his sandy blonde hair is perfectly messy. His eyes assess me, and he looks amused by what he sees.

"I was talking with Ranger and Penelope about Bridger. Did you hear? They've taken him." I'm all talk, and I mentally kick myself.

"Who's taken him? Where?" His eyes are on fire, and I feel their heat. I want to run back into the hallway and start over. Instead, I tell him what I know.

"And what were you and Chimney thinking, coming after me like you did?" I kick myself again. My accusatory tone hangs like a frayed live wire in the space between us.

"I . . . we . . ."

"I'm sorry!" I blurt, barely able to stand myself anymore. "I'm sorry and I'm grateful to you—so grateful!— but you could have died! Both of you could have died, and then what would I do?" Through blurred vision I see Nick leave his bed and step toward me.

"Celeste!" He throws his arms around me and I sink against him. "We didn't! We didn't die! We had to find you! I had to find you."

My tears soak his chest and he rocks me gently until I finally stop crying. I'm exhausted, I'm hungry, I can't believe I have any tears left—and I'm in love.

"Tell me. Tell me how you found me. I need to know everything." I want him to mention the kiss again.

He tells me everything he remembers, but when he gets to the part about the black hermit crabs and the water tunnels, I recall my own fall from the sky and baffling delivery to Kumugwe's castle—and a startling image of each god growing weaker outside his natural realm surfaces to the forefront of my consciousness.

"Kumugwe's trapped on an island and Odin's trapped in Kumugwe's castle underwater!" I blurt, jumping back from the warmth of Nick's arms. I'm such an idiot.

Nick looks at me, baffled. He knows nothing of what I've endured since I threw the Spear of Sorrow into the water and disappeared into Odin's ethereal realm.

And then I feel them before I see them. Odin's ravens are on their way.

~ 11 ~

"HIS RAVENS! They're coming! I have to get outside!" I leave Nick standing in the bedroom and run outside. Every nerve in my body tingles and I feel like I'm losing myself. Huginn and Muninn had trapped me before in the powerful force field between their wing tips and nearly prevented my escape from Odin's realm. If it hadn't been for Noor's feather-scorching rescue, I'd probably still be trapped in Asgard.

And I never would have ended up in Kumugwe's castle, and I never would have learned about Zoya's torture, and I never would have been able to help free her from Sharon's wicked parents.

Why me?

All eyes are on me when I run out the door. "Hide!" I shout to them as I scan the sky for trouble. Without questioning me, everyone scatters but Dad and Ranger, who rush to my side—my defenders. They follow my gaze and watch as two black specks in the sky grow larger.

"What are they?" Dad whispers.

"Odin's ravens. Last time I saw them they were trying to capture me." Something about their approach this time feels different, though. "Odin is trapped underwater. They feel . . . lost."

"You must hide too. They cannot take you away again." Ranger circles me, whining softly before barking at the approaching birds.

I can't recall hearing him bark before, and the noise seems to startle him as well. I remind myself that he is, in fact, a dog—a dog who once led a hungry pack on a chase to run me down for what would have been a meager meal—and who ultimately became my trainer, my guide, my protector.

"Yes! Ranger's right," Dad says. "Let's get to the house quickly."

"No, I won't hide. You go," I tell them before taking flight. I'm not about to let Odin's messengers hurt anyone in the village. I hear my father call my name. He's afraid for me, but I'm not. Not anymore.

The ravens falter in their approach when they see me blasting toward them, and just as I'm about to stretch out my hands to touch them—to let them know they have no power over me anymore—the tingling takes over and I dissolve around them. It happens quickly, just as it had that first time I dissolved in Kumugwe's castle and when I spread through the atmosphere in search of Noor on the other side.

It feels like my body is melting, multiplying, falling apart but becoming stronger, as if each tiny particle contains all of me.

It was alarming before. This time, though, I'm not afraid.

Almost as quickly as I surround them, particles of me enter through the birds' eyes and into their minds and I know they're not coming to threaten me or the villagers. This knowledge calms me. I snap back together, back into the body of Celeste, my body—a body I finally feel I have some control over—and guide the birds down to the village where

Dad nervously strokes the stubble on his chin and Ranger growls deep and low.

"It's all right, Ranger, they're not here to cause trouble." I don't have to be in Ranger's mind to understand his discomfort. Huginn and Muninn are each about twice his size, and the potential threat of their sharp, glistening beaks is very real.

Nick runs from the house toward the birds wielding a shovel, and I stop him with a word. It's just a "no," but its sound reverberates throughout the village. People peer from windows and I feel a little embarrassed for stopping him so abruptly, so loudly, so . . . powerfully. The word came from me, but in a voice I finally recognize as my true voice.

I take a deep breath.

"They're just lost, Nick." Not physically, of course, but mentally. Emotionally. Animals, fish, birds, they all feel things, remember things. I know this because I felt it in the ravens, I've witnessed it with Ranger, and I experienced it with Zoya.

Nick lowers the shovel, but keeps a firm grip on it, and movement from across the field distracts me. It's Thunder, bounding from the forest toward us, with a blurry three-headed being at his side followed by an enormous metal horse with what appears to be peacock feathers trailing behind it.

Somehow, none of this surprises me.

My reunion with Thunder is joyful! He licks my dirty face and nearly knocks me over as he rubs the length of his swirling Easter-egg-spotted coat against me. I'm introduced to the newcomers—Merts, a three-headed archer, and Lou and Layla, the spectacular fusion of peacock and horse.

For several moments, I let the ravens flutter around nervously. I let them experience a touch of fear, even, not because I want to be mean, but because I want to add to their understanding of life on a mortal planet.

"Eenie and the cubs?" I ask, and he tells me how beautiful they all are.

"Sleepin' the day away, fat an' happy, just like they're s'posed to be," he says. "Me and my peculiar posse here were just out lookin' to keep trouble away." Thunder turns his attention to the ravens, and they jump back several paces.

I'm reminded of the day I rescued Thunder from the fissure, but I don't want to think about all the tragedies that followed.

"What's up with the squawkers, little dude?" he asks, nodding toward the ravens, and I notice Merts examining the feathers on their arrows. I'm mesmerized by the archers. Their shared body appears to come in and out of focus, as if it's trying to adjust its camouflage with each passing moment. The fletchings on their arrows are identical to Odin's raven's feathers.

"They're Odin's messengers," I explain. "They travel around the planet every day and bring back thoughts and memories to him. Odin's trapped underwater right now, so they're kind of lost. They don't really have a purpose without him."

Nick stares at me while I explain, as if seeing me for the first time. I'm a mess, I know, but that's not what I see in his eyes. I see . . . admiration? Fear? No, he doesn't fear me, but there's something else I can't identify.

"Ah, Celeste?" my father whispers, touching my shoulder tentatively. "You're . . . glowing."

I look down at my hands and feet and understand why Nick and several others are wide-eyed. My copper-colored skin is radiating an emerald green glow, much like my footsteps did in the cave. It feels warm and cool. It feels electrifying. It feels powerful.

"It's okay, Dad. It doesn't hurt." They haven't seen me dissolve yet.

"But, are you ill? I've never seen you like this before." He presses his lips to my forehead, checking for fever like Mom used to do, but finding nothing out of the ordinary.

"No, I'm fine, really. It's just something that started with the fluxes. And it's helpful! Remember, Nick? It helped us find our way in the dark cave."

Nick nods slowly and I notice an inward focus, as if he's trying to remember all that happened after he and Chimney found me.

"Let's see why Huginn and Muninn came to find me." Before I return to the birds, though, the beings called Merts approach and take my hands.

"You are more than girl / Destined for discovery / Beyond this planet." It's the first time I've heard them speak, and I'm enthralled by the melody created by their combined voices. It's almost as beautiful as Harmony's voice when she's not angry or frightened.

Dad looks at me with sorrow in his eyes before questioning Merts. "What do you mean, more than girl? Don't you think she's been through enough? Don't you think we've all been through enough?" His voice cracks and he pulls me gently into a protective embrace. His agitation is contagious. The ravens hop about pecking at each other and the animals pace in circles around us.

"It's okay, Dad," I repeat. "They're not to blame for anything. I've already discovered things beyond our planet. Maybe they know this." I look at Merts to see if they agree with my interpretation, but their expressions haven't changed at all. I can't read them. "The ravens will know more. Let's find out."

I pull away from Dad gently, and he releases me slowly, reluctantly, and I approach the birds. Nick follows me, shovel still in hand.

"If they make one threatening move," he whispers.

"They won't," I say, "but thanks for being with me."
They better not do anything threatening. I don't know what
might happen if Nick tries to stop time again. I'm actually a
little surprised he didn't do it when he first saw the massive
ravens.

When I'm an arm's length from them, I open my eyes
wide. They stare into each of my eyes, sharing with me
thoughts and memories meant for Odin. I'm stunned. They've
been circling the planet and witnessing its transformation
since I threw the spear and the water receded. I feel myself
drift into their world.

~ ~ ~ ~ ~

*Copper-colored people and animals and creatures of every
sort are repopulating the land and rebuilding destroyed
villages around the planet, but vegetation pushes up too
slowly from dried, cracked mud.*

*Skirmishes break out—there's violence and bloodshed—
as fear, hunger, misunderstandings, and impatience bring out
selfish motivations.*

Why is there still fear?

*Muninn transfers memories of the ooze and the fissures
that killed or trapped nearly everyone. Those who were
trapped and kept alive underwater somehow, like my father
and possibly Thunder's peculiar posse, retain a subconscious
memory of their entrapment.*

*They're afraid it could happen again. They're afraid
they'll never feel in control of anything again.*

*And their fear is tearing them apart rather than bringing
them together.*

~ ~ ~ ~ ~

"Celeste. Celeste!" Nick's voice cuts through my trance. He shakes me gently until I'm able to break my connection with the ravens. There's wonder in his eyes when I'm finally able to look at him, and I hear him gasp.

Emotionally drained, I walk away from him and my father and friends. How will I tell them—should I tell them what I've just seen?

~ 12 ~

"WHAT'S WRONG? Why are you all staring at me?" They've followed me to where I sit on the steps in front of a house I once thought would be my new home. My head feels fuzzy and my eyesight's blurry, but I can see Huginn and Muninn circling far above us. My cheeks feel wet, so I might have been crying.

"Your eyes," Nick's voice trembles. "They're like the ravens'."

"Like the ravens'?" The words don't make any sense, so I feel my face. There's definitely something off about it.

"You have raven eyes, but the rest of you looks like you."

"More than just a girl—"

"Oy! Shuddup already with the riddles, would youz?" Lou, the part of Layla that's a peacock, silences Merts, and I smile.

But I suddenly feel very cold. "I'm freezing!" I say, shivering uncontrollably. It makes no sense. It's warm outside.

Nick sits by my side and I feel the warmth of his arms around me. I need to look at him, whatever his reaction might be. I need to look into his eyes and see what he sees. I turn my face to his and my mind swirls dizzyingly. A surge of heat floods my veins and I feel myself lifting from his arms, lifting away from him and everyone around me. I look at the green glow surrounding me like protective armor and I breathe deeply.

Salty mist, hints of sulfur, sun-ripened tomatoes in Teresa's garden, rotting vegetation far away, snoodles, rusting metal, bacon, wet clay, dust . . . honey-lemon muffins! I smell them all at once and I'm transported into a waking dream.

~ ~ ~ ~ ~

I fly between Huginn and Muninn, not trapped by them, but as one with them. We float through Odin's billowing nacreous clouds, brilliantly colored by a sun that always seems to stay on the horizon of the planet below us. His wolves prance across the strands of color to greet us.

"Bring him back to us," they say. They're talking to me. "If you do not, he surely will die."

"He's weak," I tell them, "but gods don't die. Do they?" Where I once was certain of this, now I'm unsure.

"He must return to Asgard soon or we all will die."

"All?" I ask. I fear for the planet below, though I don't fear for myself. "The people? The creatures below?"

"All," the wolves repeat in unison.

I'm whisked from this scene to a crumbled castle deep underwater.

"Is that you, buddy?" Odin's voice is barely audible, and I feel sorrow. It's because of me he's trapped down here, his life force dissipating like an early morning fog as the sun appears.

But no. It's not because of me. If he hadn't tried to keep me in Asgard, I wouldn't have ended up in Kumugwe's castle.

Do I tell him it's me? Is it a trick? Do I risk leaving him here to die? Do I risk the entire planet, and maybe even more, if I don't release him?

I try to say, "I'm here! It's me! I've come to help!" But only silent bubbles escape my mouth. I try pulling on the handle of the crushed door, but it turns into a squirming eel and I scream more bubbles.

Far above the water again, I look toward a distant shore and see the shriveled remains of octopus tentacles—Oh! Zoya! How horribly they abused you!—and near the beach, a large enclosed structure made of debris from the surrounding land. Bizarre bat-like creatures appear to be guarding it from above.

And then I fly again and I see a beautiful mermaid crying on the rocks of a small island mountain. She calls my name as I fly by and I'm lured back to her.

"Help me!" she cries. "My father, he's—"

Father! My father! He's alive! I have to return to him. But the ravens whisk me away and we soar over the crystal blue water. On and on we fly at a dizzying pace until we come to a place where no land can be seen, only blue, blue water swelling and rising as if a great beast were lifting itself slowly from beneath the salty surface.

"Where will it all go?" I ask my companions.

I know where water goes when it rises like this. I feel the swell of the water rising in my lungs, and the ravens' eyes stare into mine accusatorily.

There's something I still have to do . . .

~ ~ ~ ~ ~

This time it's my father's plea pulling me back. It's difficult—I want to stay here in this powerful form—but I harness the glow and bring myself back to the ground.

"Celeste! What's happening to you?" He runs to me, places his hands on my shoulders as if to keep me grounded, and looks me in the eyes. I can tell by his eyes that mine appear normal again.

Nick's mouth hangs open and the others gather around me in a wide circle. The rest of my friends have come out of hiding to join them, and the ravens continue to fly in loops far above. They're waiting for me.

"I'm changing, Dad, I know, but you shouldn't be afraid for me." I turn to my small circle of friends, old and new. "I've just witnessed how our planet is out of balance and in danger with Odin and Kumugwe powerless. That means we're at risk too. The Overleader—Sharon—and her parents, along with Blanche, have built a laboratory on land, and I know how they captured Bridger." I shiver at the thought of those hideous leather-winged creatures carrying him off.

"How? Where is he? When can we go get him? And can we get Blanche back too? She's not very nice, but I miss my sister." Chimney's twitching is exacerbated by excitement and impatience. It looks like he's trying to squirm out of his skin.

"Come here, Chim," I open my arms to him and he runs to me. He's grown some, but he's still a boy in need of a hug. My heart lightens when I see Orville and Riku approach.

"It won't be as easy as going to get them," I tell those in the growing circle as more people join from the village. I tell them what I know about the army they've been creating. I tell them about Harmony, discarded daughter of the malevolent scientists, who lured me into a magical sandcastle and ultimately transformed into the sad creature trying to reunite with Kumugwe, the god who raised her. I tell them about my imprisonment and the tragic fate of Zoya.

"And then you," I ruffle Chimney's hair, "and Nick came to rescue me!" I flush again at the memory of how Nick woke me up.

"So, when can we go get them?" Chimney repeats, breaking the somber mood I've created.

I gaze around at the expectant faces.

"First, I need to figure out a way to release the gods back to their realms. After that—"

"But you're just a—"

"No, she ain't, and don't youz even say it!" Lou's snarky voice stops the protester, who's probably thinking what many of them are thinking. I look at Lou and smile, and Layla bows her head to me. I stroke her metal muzzle, and she seems to feel it.

"Thanks, Lou," I say. The glow I've kept harnessed seeps beyond my skin and I know how Chimney must feel when he gets twitchy. I release it, allowing it to surround me, and I feel myself float just above the dusty ground. Everyone but those who know me best step back a pace, and even my closest friends look at me with awe.

"As I was saying, I'll free the gods because their powers can keep the planet in balance, and we'll find a way to bring Bridger home."

"And my sister too, right?"

"And Blanche too, Chim."

But what if she doesn't want to come home?

Though the urge to fly away is great, I can't leave just yet. An army like none has experienced before will be on its way here soon. I'll help them plan. So I harness my glow again, land softly in the green particles of dust I've created, and walk to where Orville stands smiling at me. The crowd parts to let me pass through them.

"Orville, our village needs a leader for what's coming. Will you do it?"

He looks at Riku, who nods gently. His smiling face transforms from an expression of surprise to one of gracious acceptance. "*Oui, ma petite,*" he says. "I will do this because you have asked."

I look over to Nick and our eyes meet. He smiles and opens his arms to me, and I go to him.

"You're not gonna go turn all green on me, are you?" he says. "Not that I'm saying it's a bad color on you—"

"I can't promise I won't," I say.

Huginn and Muninn caw loudly above us, stealing our attention away from one another. They're calling me to join them.

But they'll have to wait.

~ 13 ~

ORVILLE CALLS FOR a village meeting after Last Meal, and Nick remains with his arms around me until the crowd disperses.

"I guess I shouldn't be calling you Pipsqueak anymore." He's fidgety, playing with my dirty hair.

"It's okay. I don't mind it." I actually like it. It's his name for me.

"Whatever this thing is that's happening to you, I wanna be here for you. Unless you don't want me hanging around you anymore." He pulls me even closer, his heartbeat against mine.

"Are you kidding me? I wouldn't even be here right now if you hadn't come looking for me!" He looks me in the eyes again and I melt a little. Doesn't he know it was my desire to return to him that kept me focused on escaping from Odin and Kumugwe?

"Instead of stopping time, I wish I could turn it back to before the ooze and the fissures and all this destruction."

"But then we never would have met," I whisper.

"Yeah, I guess that's right. But you're so different. I mean, the way you glow, and your voice—it's a little scary. And really awesome. And I'm just the same."

"No, you're wrong. None of us is just the same. And your power is getting stronger. Don't you feel it?" I want him—no, I need him to believe in himself like I finally believe in me. He has to if he's going to stand up to the threat facing the members of our village. He has to if he's going to help me stay grounded.

I may not be just a girl, but I'm still a girl.

Nick contemplates what I've just asked. His pupils dilate—his mind is somewhere else—and then he looks at me again.

"Yes. I do feel stronger, but mostly because of you." He runs a hand through the disaster of a mop on my head and I'm painfully self-conscious. Then he takes my scarf from his pocket—my once beautiful emerald silk scarf, stained now with his blood and mine—and reaches behind me to tie it in a loose knot around my hair. His breath warms my cheek.

I want to cry.

"Hey," he says, lifting my chin, and just when I think he might kiss me, just when I so painfully want him to kiss me, Chimney runs from a house toward us yelling, "Last Meal! Orville says Last Meal's early today!"

The spell is broken, but the butterflies low in my belly are hungry for something more than snoodles and sun-ripened tomatoes. I've been holding my breath, and when I let it out, it releases in a silly giggle. Nick giggles too, and before I know it, Chimney is laughing with us, though he doesn't know why.

It's been too long since we've heard laughter. It's been too long since we've laughed. I step away from Nick and throw my arms around Chimney.

"I haven't properly thanked you for coming to my rescue, Chim. I owe you, buddy. It must've been scary." The word *buddy* reminds me of Odin, but he and his circling ravens will have to wait a little while longer.

"A little scary, maybe, but it was pretty cool. Those water tunnels were fun, but I don't remember how we got in 'em. Orville was s'pose to come with us too, but I guess he changed his mind. That part's fuzzy. The only time I was kinda scared was when I didn't know we could breathe in the water. I held my breath till I couldn't anymore, and then it was awesome. Makes me want to go back in the water. Can we go? Oh, and then when we went whooshing through the water, well, that was a little scary too, cuz I didn't know when we'd stop and my stomach was all upside down. Hey, were you guys gonna kiss?"

Nick looks into my eyes and raises one eyebrow, and we laugh again in an attempt to deflect the question.

"Cuz that's how Nick woke you up. Remember?" Chimney is persistent. Even though he's more than just a little boy, he's still the quirky, verbose young man who once wanted to disappear most of the time.

"Yes, smarty-pants, I remember." How could I ever forget? "And maybe we were, maybe we weren't! So, what's for Last Meal?" I ask the question to get him off the topic of kissing, and although I don't really feel hungry, I suspect I should eat something.

"Lotsa stuff from Teresa's garden and some kinda meat Merts brought back. You should see them with those magic arrows! They don't talk much, but boy, they sure can hunt. C'mon. We need to hurry up so we can find out how to bring back Bridger and Blanche."

If only it could be as easy as going to get them. Based on what Ranger's new partner Penelope shared, there are unknown ruthless beings roaming around in the outlands. Sharon and her parents would be sure to recruit them for their purposes, and based on what they did to Zoya, they're not working on ways to advance our new civilization.

And then there's the threat in the air. Evidently Orville, Noor, and I aren't the only ones who can fly. Teresa's doves are too tame for battle, and Odin's ravens, who are growing impatient with me, will return with him to Asgard once he's released. Or will they? And where's Noor?

"Hey! You comin'? Or should I leave so you two can kiss again?" Chimney scrunches up his face when he says "kiss."

"Nope! No kissing allowed before Last Meal," I say, trying to make a joke. Chimney runs back toward the house, Nick takes my hand, and we follow.

"Little guy's tough," he says. "Hardly ever complains, and I can't remember the last time he disappeared."

"What if Blanche doesn't want to come home, Nick? He'd be crushed."

"She might not. But he has us. He has a family. He'll be all right." Nick stops at the porch steps and pulls me into another embrace. "I was afraid I'd lost you, Celeste."

The door opens and I smell something delicious.

"I'm here," I say, wishing time would stop.

~ ~ ~ ~ ~

I slip away once we get into the house. My mother used to say there were "too many cooks in the kitchen" during holiday meal preparation, and now I understand what she meant. If she were in this kitchen today, though, I'd be right by her side whether she needed my help or not.

"Be right back," I tell Nick, and I'm happy to find no one in the bathroom upstairs. I remember Lena's "quick like a bunny" comment the first time I showered in this house. The water was barely warm then, and now it's just cold. But I don't care. It feels so good to wash off a layer of salt and grime. Someone has managed to create a bottled substance resembling soap—I suspect Maddie and Teresa combined their talents—and I'm grateful for it.

I do my best to wash the stains from my scarf, but only the dirt flows down the drain. The blood stains are there forever. I'm okay with that. Orville may have said "never forever" a lifetime ago, but blood is forever. So many memories in this house.

My clothes are damaged beyond repair and smell like they look. What happens to them when I disperse? And what happened to them when I became a dove? The question amuses me, because somehow, I always end up back in them when I become Celeste again. It's like my clothes hang around to remind me I'm human, to bring me back to myself.

I can't bear to put them back on.

I run across the hall to a room Maddie shares with Teresa and search through their closet. There's not much to choose from, but there's a simple dress pushed far to the side.

A dress. The last dress I recall wearing was on Easter morning. I was probably eight. They're not very practical, dresses, but this one has pockets, and for some reason, I really want to wear it. It fits like it was waiting for me to put it on.

I remember the apples and core in the pockets of my filthy clothes and put them in these clean pockets. I tie back my hair with my damp scarf and join those gathered for Last Meal downstairs.

~ **14** ~

NICK SITS at the bottom of the stairs as I descend, and when he looks up at me, his mouth opens as wide as his eyes. I laugh, and he closes his mouth quickly, but his eyes don't change. He jumps up and steps back to let me by.

"You look beautiful," he says, and I'm not self-conscious anymore. I feel beautiful, and it's not just because of the dress. It's not even just because of how I see myself through his eyes. It's because of something deep inside me, something finally coming to the surface. Something I'm finally accepting about myself.

"Thanks. I guess it's been a while since you've seen me clean." I don't count the time he found me floating in an underwater tube.

"Well, will you look at my girl," Dad says to the group in the kitchen, and I become the topic of conversation while we eat. All the attention makes me a little uncomfortable, but it's the kind of attention I haven't had for as long as I can remember. It's the good kind.

"The dress looks wonderful on you," Teresa says. "I'm happy you found it. It's yours."

I thank her for it and smile. Is Mac ever *not* by her side? He looks at her the way Nick is starting to look at me, and I can tell it makes her feel the same way I feel—all warm inside, and safe. Teresa has her own glow, not green like mine, but a more natural one. Despite the constant uncertainty of the world we're living in, she seems happy.

Maybe happiness is as simple as having someone to love.

"Oh! Before I forget," I say, retrieving the apples. "For your garden! I found these on a tree from the other side."

Teresa's eyes light up. It's been ages since anyone on this side has eaten an apple, and she'll have trees growing in no time.

"And now will you tell us where you've been?" she asks.

I share abbreviated stories of the dining hall in Asgard and how I once landed in an enormous bread bowl after one of my fluxes, and everyone laughs. I tell them about the great vat of eyeballs in Kumugwe's castle.

"Really, Celeste? You want us thinking about vats of eyeballs while we're eating?" Lena looks at me disapprovingly and I want to laugh—she's too young to have mastered the expression of chastisement on her face—but she's right.

"Yeah, Celeste," her twin, Katie, agrees. "But I bet Jack would eat them!"

"Sure, I'd eat 'em! They probly make you strong," says Jack, flexing his skinny arms and making everyone laugh again. I'd forgotten about the boy's speed and strength. "Maybe me and Nick woulda found you sooner if we ate eyeballs too!"

The twins laugh—it's clear they enjoy Jack's antics—and Jack tells me about his boating adventure with Nick when Harmony had held me captive another lifetime ago, before I even knew who she was. This boy risked his life to find me too.

And Harmony was just a song to me then—a lovely, lilting child's song.

"Sorry! I probably shouldn't be talking about that while we're eating, but to the copper god, they're like treats!"

Everyone groans, and Mac says, "Enough with the eyeballs, already!"

"The copper god, you say?" Teresa caresses Mac's cheek as if pointing out the obvious. "Is he the reason we all have copper skin?"

"I'm not sure. Kumugwe doesn't seem to care much about what happens topside as long as his underwater world is safe. Would you please pass the eyeba—I mean, the potatoes, Jack?"

"Good one, Celeste!" Jack jumps up to pass a bowl of small, round potatoes to me. "Save a couple more for me too!"

"And me three!" says Lena.

"And me four!" says Katie.

Even Dad laughs, though I catch him looking at me with concern in his eyes throughout the meal. It can't be easy for him, knowing he could lose me again so soon after finding me. But I'm confident it won't take me long to release Kumugwe. And then we'll set Odin free.

"Who'd you like best, Celeste, Odin or Kumugwe? I'm gonna guess Kumugwe." Jack is obviously enthralled by the eyeball-eating water god.

The question takes me by surprise.

"You know, I liked certain things about both of them." It's an evasion, but after escaping from the battling brothers, I hadn't really considered the idea of liking either of them.

"Like what things?" Lena asks, and Katie repeats the question. I love how they support one another, each with her unique, special power, neither one ever trying to outdo the other. How lucky to be born with someone you'll share a bond with forever.

I can see they're not going to let me off easy on this.

"What things? Well, Odin's really just looking for someone to help him with his chores, and he taught me how to make rain. I liked that." I feel a tingle of power when I recall drawing the water up from a lake and releasing it over a mountain range, and my hands start to glow. I pull it back. I have to stay grounded, at least through dinner. "And his food was the best. You can't even imagine the meats and cheeses and breads and treats on his table every evening."

"Did he have mint chocolate chip ice cream?" Jack's eyes grow wide when he asks, and I remember a time when every freezer had ice cream.

"And bananas with honey?" Maddie's question makes me wonder what happened to the bees.

And will we ever figure out how to restore power and bring light back into our lives and into our homes again? I feel a little guilty for having mentioned these delicacies, but everyone looks hungry for more details.

"Yes, every flavor of ice cream and bananas with honey and whatever I asked for. Odin would have given me anything I wanted just to keep me there with him. He was pretty lonely." Saying it makes me sad for him.

"Maybe he should come live with us!" Chimney suggests. "Betcha he didn't have snoodles up there in the clouds!"

His suggestion is dismissed with laughter, but it plants a seed in my brain.

"What about Kumugwe?" Jack snaps back from his ice cream reverie.

"Let's see. Kumugwe taught me I could breathe underwater, and he loves his sea creatures, so I like those things about him." I'm not telling the young ones about the horrors I discovered when he released me to find Zoya. "And he rescued a little girl and raised her like she was his own daughter." The more I talk about the gods, the more I realize they may not be the monsters I was beginning to think they were.

"Perhaps the villagers should learn more about these gods too?" Orville glances around the table and it's clear we're near the end of our meal. "I hear them gathering outside."

"Yes! And I have more technical things to share with them." I pause for a moment and look at the young faces around the table. Chimney, Jack, Lena, and Katie look at me with raised eyebrows, waiting for me to tell them more about the gods, but I don't want them to hear what I have to tell the villagers.

"Maddie, do you have a new story to share," I nod subtly toward the youngsters, "while I talk to the people outside about some really boring stuff?"

Maddie smirks at me. I know she wants to be included with the more mature members of the village, but she understands. "Do I have a story? You can't even imagine the story I'm going to share, but it's only for these guys. Sorry, but the rest of you have to go outside now." With that, Maddie hurries out of the kitchen toward the room where she used to teach the children, and they run right behind her.

"Those kids are pretty strong," Nick says, "but it's nice of you to give them a little break from all the heaviness. Last Meal was fun. It's great to hear them laugh."

Everyone is silent for a moment as the weight of Nick's words hangs in the air. He's feeling the same thing I've just felt. We're all feeling it. It's been a memorable meal, and I don't want it to end. With my father here, these people are starting to feel like family. This place is starting to feel like home.

Dad smiles at me and nods. He feels like a stable force here among so many young people. I've missed his support and guidance—and approval—so much more than I realized.

But it's time to share the visions I've seen and the threat we face with the others. If we can't stop the scientists and their bizarre army, there may be no more Last Meals like the one we just enjoyed.

I take a deep breath and follow Orville out the door.

~ 15 ~

OVER GASPS FROM VILLAGERS when they see me in a dress, I hear the insistent call of Odin's ravens—circling impatiently—and acknowledge them with a look. The evening is mild and the setting sun paints drifting stratus clouds with fiery colors.

Nick stands by me on one side, and Chimney joins me on the other, though I hoped he would have followed Maddie with the other young ones. It was a foolish expectation. Despite missing his sister, Chimney has been his own person since the first time Orville and I encountered him on a hilltop beyond the village.

The crowd—a mixture of human and animal—is quiet, waiting for me to speak. Their expressions and postures, alert and open, tell me they're ready for whatever I'm about to share. I try to ignore the butterflies in my stomach.

"Thank you for coming together," I start. "I feel like I've been gone a long time." I see smiles and nods.

"While I've been away, I've seen things and been places I never could have imagined outside my dreams. Two old gods have tried to imprison me, and now they're both trapped and powerless. They need to be freed if we want our planet to be repaired."

I wait for the mumbling to settle down.

"As I told some of you earlier, Odin—the god you used to chant to for rain every evening—is growing weak. He's trapped in Kumugwe's underwater castle. Those are his ravens flying above." I point to them and everyone looks up. Expressions vary from wide-eyed awe to fear.

"They're not a threat to us, but they and Odin's wolves who roam in Asgard above need him back, and we need for him to be back in his realm too." This may not be completely true, but it feels right. Odin will have to decide how he's going to behave once he's released.

"But why? He didn't help us before," someone calls from the crowd.

"Yeah. And who's this Kumugwe?" someone else questions, and my answers better be convincing.

"Odin watches over more than just our little village. I can't pretend to know how he makes his decisions, but he has to look at what's best for the entire planet. And Kumugwe is god of the seas. Kumugwe calls Odin his brother. He rescued Harmony after her parents—the scientists who are creating an army and who kidnapped Bridger—threw her away into the sea. He's raised her from the time she was an infant."

"But I don't get it. Why would he want to keep that weird, scary girl?" Chimney asks, scrunching his shoulders.

They know nothing about her.

"Isn't she Sharon's sister?" Teresa asks. "I remember them walking hand in hand after the child came from the water, after you threw the spear and—"

"Disappeared," Nick finishes her sentence. He looks at me as if I might disappear again. I take his hand and squeeze it gently.

I look at Dad and he gives me an encouraging nod to continue. I feel his approval and see pride in his eyes.

"Kumugwe saw something special in her. He believed in her. He raised her and taught her everything, including how to camouflage herself, like octopuses do. He's trapped on a dry, rocky island, and Harmony swims around it, afraid. I'll release him first."

Dad looks thoughtful. "How will you do this, Celeste? If Harmony hasn't been able to free him—"

"Yeah, and now that I think about it, maybe you shouldn't even let him out," Chimney interrupts. He looks angry. "What if he's mad and traps you again, or he could send a big wave again, or a—" He fades while he talks.

I can see him clearly, but the others squint toward where they last saw him by my side. I understand the stress he feels and why he might want to disappear.

"I hear what you're saying, Chim, but I got to know him pretty well when I was there. More than anything, he really just wanted the ooze gone and Harmony back. He needs to watch after all the beings in the sea, including Harmony, and she needs her father."

Chimney reappears and nods. I feel like he understands wanting a father. Dad puts an arm around his shoulders and Chimney leans against him.

"As for how I'll release him from the rock island on the far side of the water, I know someone who might help."

Ranger's ears perk up. "The mountain spirit," he says. "Old Man Massive will help you, Celeste."

"This is my hope. The mountain spirit was the one who trapped Kumugwe when Chimney, Nick, and I were in danger in the water. Once Kumugwe's free, I'll convince him to release Odin. I'm pretty sure he'll be happy to get him out of his castle."

There are concerned expressions scattered throughout the group and several look at me with what feels like compassion in their eyes.

Orville, ever supportive of me, nods and asks, "So, where are they, these scientists? You mentioned seeing a structure. And what do you know about their army?"

I tell them about the submarine hidden inside the octopus, and how I discovered the source of the poisonous ooze coming from experiments Sharon's parents were conducting in there. I tell them about Zoya, and how I helped Harmony stop her torturous mechanical heart.

"They were creating an army of gooey automated life forms under the protection of the octopus's camouflage. The ravens showed me a vision"—it was a horrible vision, Zoya's severed limbs on a beach, squirming creatures emerging from them—"of a structure near a waterfront a distance from here, probably where they're continuing their work. Broken pieces of their submarine are scattered on the shore."

The ravens screech. I want to trust they wouldn't harm anyone here, but the sooner they have what they want, the sooner I can return and help my village defend itself. Based on the vision, the threat isn't imminent, but I can't be sure how much time I have.

I remind myself I've never had time.

I continue. "They also showed me winged, bat-like creatures, as large as the ravens themselves, several of them. They captured Bridger." I look at Chimney to judge his reaction. He still looks angry. Many in the crowd look angry too. "So you'll have to watch the sky while I'm gone."

"Merts," Orville addresses the archers, "can you equip others with bows and arrows? And quickly?"

"We will equip them / We are ready to protect / Our mission is clear." Merts signals for several people in the group to follow them into the trees. There's no hesitation.

I'm reassured by their teamwork. It didn't exist the last time I was here. Time for me to leave.

"Residents of—" I falter. I don't know the name of this village, or if it even has a name. I look around at the faces for an answer, but the reality has just dawned on them too. Shoulders shrug. I look to Orville for an answer. I've asked him to lead our people.

"Vittoria," he says. It's a humble suggestion. He waits, and when I look around once more, I see slow smiles and subtle nods.

It's perfect.

"Residents of Vittoria! With your help, Orville will develop plans for our defense. When I return, I'll know more about what we're up against. Until I do, watch the sky for the bat creatures, and take care of one another."

I hug Chimney. "Don't worry, buddy. I'll be back, quick like a bunny." He holds on for longer than I expected, and then I turn to hug my father.

"I've missed so many years of your life. Not fair, right?" He releases me quickly and lays his hands on my shoulders so he can look me in the eyes. "I don't want you to go, but I agree with your decision. You come back to me soon, daughter." His voice cracks.

"I will, Daddy," I say. "And remember, you always told me life's not fair. But it's okay."

"You come back to me." He pulls me into a tight squeeze again, then let's me go and walks away. He doesn't turn back.

I leave the group, they're already focused on Orville, and I'm not surprised to feel Nick's hand in mine again.

"I'm going with you," he says, "and you can't stop me."

~ 16 ~

"BUT YOU CAN'T! They need you here!" I want to retract my words immediately. Even if what I said is true, I just told him I didn't need him. Instead of looking defeated, though, Nick puts his hands on his hips and stands taller.

"You're not the only one with powers, Celeste, and you're not the only one who cares about saving this village."

Ouch.

"You asked Orville to be a leader, and look at him." We both look over to where Orville is talking with people and arranging them into groups—Riku helps him—and as if sensing our attention, he looks over at us. He smiles and nods, and a faint voice in my head, his voice, says, "You two go. Return with helpful news."

I hope I'll always have this connection with Orville. But when I look back at Nick and feel what his closeness does to me, I hope Orville won't be sharing my dreams anymore. That's why I want Nick to stay here. He might distract me. He does distract me.

"You're right, Nick. But you know these people better than I do, and you're the only one who can stop time if I don't make it ba—"

"Don't say it. Don't even think it. I'm going with you, and we're coming back together. You know I can breathe underwater, and you're going to need my help."

"But—" I search for another reason to keep him here. "You can't fly, and—"

"But you can, and you've carried me before without slowing down." He's agitated, his words come out like an accusation, and he pulls it back. "I'm sorry. I didn't mean to jump down your throat. What I meant to say was, thanks for the times you've carried me, especially this last time. I thought I was going to die, but I could hear your voice and feel you holding me, and I knew you'd find a way to bring me back. I need to be with you this time. I won't be able to help anyone back here if my mind is distracted with worrying about you."

So, which distraction could be the most destructive? Before I can come up with another argument for keeping him here, someone shouts, "Look out!" and all eyes turn skyward.

I fear the bats, but it's not them. It's Huginn and Muninn on a dive-bomb descent toward me and Nick. I see Nick's face change the way it does right before he stops time, but he's too late. One of the ravens grasps his shirt at the shoulders, the other grasps the bottom of his pant legs, and they're flying off with him before I can register what's just happened.

I leap to the air and chase the unwieldy, almost comical sight ahead of me, though Nick doesn't appear to be struggling. The way they're holding him, he appears to fly between them. As I gain on them, Huginn turns his head back toward me and his eyes tell me their intentions.

It was time to go. The boy was keeping me too long. It was clear to them he wanted to stay with me. They were being helpful.

When I'm alongside Nick, he turns to me and his entire face lights up. I've never seen a smile so big.

"Guess I won that one!" he shouts through the wind.

"Guess so, but you cheated!" I shout back, and our laughter fills the wake we leave behind.

We're silent for a while as we fly over miles of pristine water so clear I can recognize the creatures swimming below. How many of them were in the enormous water bubble that floated high above the sea after I threw Kumugwe's spear into the poisoned water? To me and all the villagers, the orichalcum-inlaid weapon was the Spear of Sorrow.

Just the memory of that day in the Overleader's oppressive house and the horror she made me experience makes my heart sink, and I fall down and back a little, but I shake it off. She's not the Overleader anymore, and I'm not a scared girl.

"Where'd you go?" Nick asks when I catch up with him and his bizarre entourage.

Do I tell him the truth? Does he need to know everything going through my head? Yes, and no.

"I was remembering the Spear of Sorrow and it took me by surprise, that's all. Did you know the spear belongs to Kumugwe? He was happy to get it back."

"But why did he make it so horrible?"

"He didn't. In his hands it was beautiful. Somehow Sharon changed its structure when she had it, maybe the same way she changed her own shape."

"So, it's not dangerous anymore?"

"It didn't seem like it was, but I don't know what Kumugwe uses it for. I guess any weapon can be dangerous."

We're silent again for another long stretch, and I try to get Sharon out of my head. The wind in our faces and the endless span of water below lull us into a trancelike state and time seems to expand in every direction. My flight is effortless. I tingle, and when I feel my fingertips start to dissolve, I shake myself back together and focus on the horizon. The sun is near setting and the clouds just above our heads glow muted hues of oranges and pinks, not quite as beautiful as the clouds in Asgard, but beautiful enough to admire.

Nick's voice startles me back from my quiet place. "Any idea where we're going?"

It's a good question. I've been staying with the path Huginn and Muninn are on, but they don't know I plan to rescue Kumugwe first.

"I guess I should tell them my plan," I say, and I fly closer to Huginn to get his attention. When he looks at me, I understand the ravens are planning to drop Nick into the water over the place they last saw Odin enter the sea. They know I'll follow, and we're to release Odin. They have no allegiance to Kumugwe. Evidently, we're close.

No, I tell them. *Kumugwe is the one with the power to release Odin from his collapsed castle, not us. We're going to the island on the far side of the water first. Odin will be safe until then.*

Huginn balks and caws for Muninn's attention, and while the ravens communicate, our forward progress stalls.

"What's wrong?" Nick looks from one bird to the other, and then below to the water, before looking back at me. "They're not gonna drop me this high up, are they? I mean, I know I'll be okay once I'm in the water, but this is really, really high up and—"

"They better not, but if they do, I'll catch you." I tell him what Huginn relayed to me, and then Nick surprises me.

"Hey! You two! You'll do what Celeste tells you to do or you'll never see your cherished Odin again. We'll make sure of that. Do you hear me?"

I smile.

The ravens flutter about for a moment and Nick is jostled between them. I'm ready to dive for him if they're foolish enough to release him, but they don't.

"To the island!" I tell them, and after they stare at me for a moment with their steely black eyes, a failed attempt at intimidating me, they resume their northward flight with Nick secure between them.

"Guess we both won that one!" I try not to stare at Nick as we soar over the water, but I can't help it. Everything about him makes me want to be closer to him.

It's a distraction I'll enjoy while I can.

~ 17 ~

I SEE A BUMP on the horizon just as the last bit of sun slips from sight. Nick is getting fidgety and I can't say I blame him. The ravens haven't been flying as gracefully since their censure, and I'm certain it's been on purpose. What will we find when we land?

"There!" I point to the island.

"Please let them know how upset you'll be if they drop me onto those rocks," Nick says, and I'm happy to know he hasn't lost his sense of humor. Now that we've arrived, I can't imagine being here without him. It's been a long flight with the sulky ravens.

"Easy!" I direct the birds when we reach the edge of the island. "Feet first," I tell Huginn, and when he lets go, Nick dangles beneath Muninn, who still holds him by the shoulders. "Down slowly, Muninn. Gently!" Nick is safely on the ground, though his legs look a little wobbly.

"Never thought I'd be so happy to feel my feet on the ground again," he says, raising his hands up to me like he's ready to catch me if I happen to fall this last short distance. I think about doing just that, imagining how it would feel to have him catch me.

Just as I'm ready to take his hands, though, a splashing in the sea just beyond where Nick stands distracts me, and I watch in surprise as Harmony—dazzlingly opalescent—propels herself from the water with her great tail and grabs Nick from the shoreline, pulling him back into the water with her. His startled shout is muffled by bubbles as she pulls him under deeper than I can see.

I don't land, but dive in after them. A sick feeling in my stomach frightens me—what's she doing? Where is she taking him? Why?

The glow from Harmony's tail tells me where they are in the dark water ahead of me.

"Harmony! Stop!" I shout through the salty surroundings, willing myself to swim faster.

She stops and spins around to face me. Nick looks perplexed, but he appears to be breathing okay.

"You can't have him until you bring my father back to me, and if he's hurt, your boy will be hurt too."

Hearing her words, Nick struggles to free himself, but Harmony is twice his size, and the hold she has on him is far too strong.

"Remember, Celeste, Kumugwe gave me many powers. We decide who among those with pure intentions can breathe in our world." She swooshes her hand in front of Nick's face and I see his eyes grow wide. He struggles frantically in her grasp as bubbles escape his mouth. His copper-colored skin fades to white and he searches for me in the darkness. If I don't stop her, his next breath will be his last.

"Harmony, stop! You're not like your birth parents! You're not a murderer! Let him breathe! Now!" My heart constricts, I hold my breath—I've never felt more powerless—how could I have allowed this to happen?

She looks at Nick fighting to free himself from her arms, fighting to hold the last swallow of oxygen in his lungs before inhaling a breath of death, and an expression beyond sorrow washes over her. She swooshes her hand once more and he is safe. He collapses motionless in her arms, but his color has returned and he's breathing.

I exhale, and every particle in my body vibrates. I feel like I might explode, and in an instant, I close the distance between us and grab Nick from her arms, leaving her crying a melody I recall from the time Orville rescued me from her sandcastle.

The sound is achingly beautiful and impossible to describe, even more beautiful than when the three heads of Merts speak together.

"You keep leaving me, Celeste. Why do you keep leaving me? Why does everyone keep leaving me? I heard you in the sky above—you saw me, I know it—and you left me here swimming around the island. And I can't hear him anymore! What if he's gone now too? What if Kumugwe has left me all alone?"

I'm moved to tears with her—the sea is filled with tears! And even though Harmony has camouflaged herself to look like a woman, emotionally and intellectually she's probably only about seven. She's still a girl. A large, powerful, beautiful girl with a very long tail.

With Nick unconscious in one arm, I open my other to Harmony, and she accepts my awkward embrace. I don't tell her how worried I am about her comment. What could it mean if she can't hear Kumugwe anymore? And what will happen if the copper god is dead?

"Nick will be okay, right?" I'm far more concerned about him than I am about the ancient god.

"Yes," Harmony tells me. "He's asleep. The struggles and the fright used all the energy in his body. He'll be better after he sleeps. I'm sorry, Celeste. That was a wicked thing to do. I'm not a wicked girl. And did you know my birth father recognized me? He wouldn't now, but he did in the submarine."

Harmony cries again before continuing. "Poor Zoya! Poor, poor Zoya! Those are the wicked ones! And they left me again! This boy and a smaller one were in a water tube, and I was pulling it away from the submarine so they wouldn't see us—I was going to stop them, Celeste, I was!—and they left me! Why didn't Sharon stop them?"

"I can't answer that, Harmony." I'll have to wait before asking her the countless questions filling my brain. "Let's go to the island and free Kumugwe." I'm surprised by how much I want him to be alive.

Harmony leads me back to the island, and I carry Nick onto the rocky shore and find a flat place to lay him down.

"Holy moly!" I yell when I turn back around to the water, startled to find Harmony standing right behind me. "How'd you—"

"I've walked all over this island and I can't find a way in," she says.

Of course she can have legs if she wants them. She's been learning how to camouflage her body since she was an infant.

I know what I'm about to ask is risky. "Harmony, I have to take a really short flight, just right over there to where you can see land." I'm grateful for my night vision. "I have to leave Nick here. There's an old friend there who can help us move these rocks and free your father. Are you okay with me doing that?"

She takes a long time to answer.

"You'll be back fast?"

"Yes, as fast as I can."

"You're not leaving me here alone for a long, long time?"

"No, of course not. And I can't leave Nick alone, so you have to watch him while I'm gone."

She hesitates, looking from me to Nick and back to me again before nodding. "Okay. But what do I tell him if he wakes up?"

"First, tell him you're sorry for scaring him like you did and you'll never do it again. Then, tell him I'm getting Old Man Massive to help. He'll understand."

"Okay," she whispers, and walks over to sit by Nick's side.

"I'll return soon and everything will be okay. Okay?"

"Promise?"

She's just a child.

"Promise," I say.

With all my heart, I hope the mountain spirit is awake and can do what I need him to do. If not—no, I can't think about that. I leap into the air and am over his crumbled profile in an instant.

~ **18** ~

OLD MAN MASSIVE collapsed himself to prevent Nick, Chimney, and me from crashing into his wall, and I hardly recognize him in the rubble. I land on his nose, ever prominent in the heap.

"The boy. Did he make it?" The mountain spirit opens his great eye as soon as my feet touch down. The boom of his voice shifts loose boulders into new places and for a moment I flinch, ready to fly to safety if one of them tumbles my way.

"Yes! We all made it, thanks to you." I want to hug him, but how would I hug a mountain?

"You have come for help, yes?"

"Yes again. And I hope someday not to have to disturb you from your slumber. I'd really enjoy a boring visit with you at some point. Not that you're boring! That's not what I meant! What I meant was—"

"I know what you are saying, little dove, and I am honored. Good that you have come. I would not release the water god until I was certain this is what you would want. I fear, however, it may be too late."

"No! I mean, yes, it's what I want, and no, it can't be too late! Why too late?"

"The wailing of the child, though glorious, has grown louder while the raving of the god has stopped. Tell me you will be safe and I will open the island to the sea."

"I'll be safe. Kumugwe has no control over me anymore, but wait! Nick and Harmony are on the island." I explain what's just happened, and Nick's condition.

"He endangers himself yet again. He is true." Old Man Massive whispers the last words, and I feel guilty for having put Nick in another predicament. As if sensing my anguish, Old Man Massive continues. "As you have been marked to endure countless trials, so too is he destined for a future unknown to us. You are not responsible for his actions."

"But if it weren't for me, he'd be safe right now."

"Would he, though? This, we cannot know. Return to the island, child, and shout my name to the sky. I will hear you, and I will release the sea god—however he may fare—back to his realm."

"This is another sad goodbye, then, because I'll have to return quickly to the village on the other side once the gods are back where they belong."

"Why sad, little one? Does not your father wait for you?"

"Yes! He's there! Sorry I questioned you when you told me it was him. But he and my friends are still in danger. Tell me, old friend, has the planet always been in turmoil?"

"My answer will not matter. Go, and call my name when you are prepared. I will be here when you return, whenever that may be. Remember who you are, Celeste, and remember what you have learned."

Have I learned anything? Of course I have. I've learned that in an instant, lives can be torn apart for no sensible reason. I've learned there are people on the planet who do stupid things because they're afraid, and people who do horrible things because they're horrible.

But there are people—not just people, other beings as well—who do extraordinary things too. They're the ones who need to be stronger than the bad beings. They're the ones who need to work together to survive, to rebuild, to overcome challenges that might never make sense.

I'm one of those, and I'll use every power in this ever-changing body to help these new survivors defeat those who want them to suffer more than they already have.

"I'll remember, Old Man. And I won't let you down. You'll see me again. Listen for my call soon, and thank you." I kneel down and plant a kiss on his enormous, dusty nose. I thought it might feel silly, but it doesn't, and the mountain spirit moves his cracked stone lips into a gentle smile.

Flying back to the island in the cool darkness, I experience a feeling I can only describe as euphoria. I tingle, I glow, and the air surrounding me feels electric.

When I get to the island, Nick is just starting to move and Harmony is humming a quiet melody by his side. She's a beautiful girl, really; her long pink hair falls in waves down her back and her copper skin glows softly. She jumps up and runs to me when I land.

"Will your friend help? Will he help us find my father?"

"Yes. He's just waiting for me to call his name."

"What are you waiting for?" Harmony pulls at my dress. "Hurry!"

I run to Nick and jostle him. "Nick, wake up." He's groggy. Harmony paces in tight circles looking over to where I'm shaking him, and then she stomps her feet on the ground.

"Hurry!" she shouts.

Her voice hurts my ears and the ground she stomps upon rumbles. She starts to grow in size, though she still looks like a child, and I don't know what she might do next.

"Wha . . . what the . . ."

"Nick! Get up! And Harmony, calm down!" I turn around to see her looming over us, a giant of a child, and I put my hand up to stop her. From what, I'm not sure, because she's just standing there looking petulant, but then I see Nick's face changes and I can't let it happen again.

"No! Nick, it's all right. Do *not* stop time! You're with me and we're going to release Kumugwe. You're okay. Now, get up!"

He finally focuses on me, I'm glowing so he can see me, and he stands up.

"Not cool, Harmony," he says, rubbing his forehead. "So not cool. Why would you do that to me?"

I look up at Harmony and see she's about to cry.

"I just want my father back. I'm sorry!"

"She's just a little girl, Nick," I whisper to him. He gives me a look that says he doesn't care how old she is, she shouldn't have threatened his life as she did.

"Hey, don't cry," he says. "And promise me you'll give me a little warning next time you're about to kidnap me, okay?"

"Okay," she says, stifling her sniffles. "But could we please get my father out of this island now?"

"Yes," I say, squeezing Nick's hand. "I'll call him, but we shouldn't be standing on the island when I do. You go back to the water, Harmony, and Nick? Hold on."

We wrap our arms around each other and lift into the air. Harmony dives from where she stands, and I see her resurface a distance away. She's child-size again, with a little opalescent tail.

"Ready?" I ask, though none of us knows what to be ready for. "Block your ears," I whisper to Nick, and then I take a deep breath and call his name.

"OLD . . . MAN . . . MASSIVE!" My voice startles even me.

And then the rumbling begins.

~ 19 ~

WE CLING TO ONE ANOTHER above the splashing water, and although he can't see what's happening below—it's too dark for his eyes—Nick senses the turmoil in the atmosphere. I see what's happening. I feel his heart beating rapidly. Mine remains steady.

"Sounds like Harmony's throwing another fit," he says. "What's going on?"

"It's not her." I glance down at Harmony, who propels herself from the water over and over as the waves rise and fall in massive surges beneath us. She looks scared, but she's in her element. I'm not worried about her. "It's the mountain," I tell Nick. "He's tearing the island apart to release Kumugwe."

The boulders making up the island vibrate and I watch as they start tumbling into the water, and in the distance where the precipice has crumbled, I see the dark outline of his mountain range rising.

"Holy moly! Old Man Massive is rebuilding himself!" I watch boulder upon boulder rising from the sea. The rumbling continues and continues until there's barely anything left of the island below. The mountain range to the north has grown substantially, and finally, the waves settle.

"Whoa! I see it!" Nick says. "And I thought *we* had powers!"

In the nearly imperceptible brightening of the sky just before the first rays of sunlight break the horizon, we look to what remains of the island. On it rests a colossal, motionless shape.

It's him.

Harmony swims to the island and regains her legs just as I land with Nick in my arms. We're not eager to let go of one another, and I see him looking at the hulk on the ground with some trepidation.

"Is this really a good idea, Celeste? He doesn't look too good. What if Chimney's right and he gets angry?"

Before I can answer, Harmony's cry pierces the atmosphere. We hurry over to where she's collapsed on the ground and see the reason for her despair.

Kumugwe is a shriveled shell of the god he once was. His chest is sunken, as are the cheeks of his broad face, and what remains of his skin is stuck to his bones. The fins encircling his enormous head hang open. They look like burnt layers of paper, and his tail, his glorious tail, lies flattened against the hard ground. His eyes are closed. I can't imagine them lifeless.

His beautiful spear rests alongside him in the open palm of his right hand. I'm tempted to touch it.

"Father!" Harmony howls. "I'm here! Your little music-maker is here! Open your eyes, father! Wake up!" She tries to shake him awake, but she's so small and he's so . . .

I have an idea. "Harmony." I take her gently by the shoulders and lift her away from him. She looks so helpless, but I've seen what she can do. "Will you grow yourself big again, like you did when Nick was asleep and you walked up onto the island? We're going to carry him back into the sea, but I need your help."

His lifeless form is many times larger than Thunder was when I pulled him from the fissure wall, and Kumugwe's body looks so frighteningly fragile.

Also, I need to stop Harmony from crying. Nick stands behind me pressing his hands against his ears, and my head aches. When she's cried in the past, her sorrow has sounded hauntingly beautiful. This, though, is excruciating.

"Okay," she pouts, "but why? He's gone, isn't he? Where will I live? What will I do? How will I—"

"We need to return him to the sea." I stop her from spinning back into a frenzy. "It's the right thing to do. Your questions will have to wait. Now, help me please, will you?"

Nick scans the length and bulk of the lifeless god as if looking for a way to help. He walks over to where the spear lies loose in Kumugwe's palm, and with both hands he closes the god's fingers around it. Then, he squats down to gather the hand and forearm in his arms before standing up. Beads of sweat drip from his forehead. "Let's do this," he says.

Harmony's cry softens to a sob and she grows herself large enough to wrap her arms around Kumugwe's ribs. I wrap my arms around the narrowest part of his tail near his flukes and together, we lift his body and move in step toward the water.

The sea is surprisingly calm. The three of us tread water around his floating body, which bobs gently in the subtle swells reflecting the rising sun. We watch. We wait. And wait.

"What now?" Harmony's ready to cry again, I can hear it in her tone.

What do I tell her? Do I say, "I thought the sea would bring him back to life"? Do I say, "He's happy, back where he belongs"?

I *did* think the sea would bring him back. I *did* think the cells in his body would rehydrate once he returned to his natural element.

"I'm sorry, Harmony, I don't . . . wait!" Something in Nick's eyes reminds me of what I saw when Ryder was healing his brain. When Ryder and *I* were healing his brain. I wondered then if I could have done it on my own. It's time to answer my question. "I'm going to try something, Harmony. Don't be frightened, okay?" I swim over toward the top of Kumugwe's head. "I'll need you to hold his eyelids open for me."

"But why? He's gone! He'll never see again. He'll never see *me* again!"

"Please, Harmony, and I won't ever ask you to do anything you don't want to do again."

"Why don't you sing a nice song like you did while I was trying to wake up," Nick suggests. "It was beautiful, and I wanted to open my eyes to see who was singing."

His kindness touches me. Harmony nearly killed him, and now he's giving her strength. She smiles at him.

"You can look away if you want, but I need to look into his eyes. Can you help me do this?"

Reluctantly yet gently, Harmony lifts Kumugwe's multiple-layered eyelids from his eyes and looks away quickly. She starts to hum an entrancing tune, softly at first, and then with growing conviction.

I mouth the words *thank you* to Nick, and his smile warms the chill I feel when I consider what I'm about to try.

I position myself so I can look directly into Kumugwe's filmy eyes. The mark on my head tingles as I focus, and I feel my glow warm the water around us. I can't tell if I'm dissolving, but some of my particles have crossed the physical boundary between me and the water god, and I understand what's happened to the cells in his body.

They've closed down on themselves like deflated balloons.

Instinctively, my body soaks up water until my cells are saturated. It's almost like how I felt when I absorbed the liquid from Nick's brain, but this time in reverse.

Harmony's song is a soothing, distant echo.

What a bizarre feeling. When my particles can't hold anymore, my cells constrict and force the salty sea-water into Kumugwe's collapsed cells. This happens again and again— I'm like a pump—and the cells in his body respond. Tiny glimmers spread through his body as each cell comes back to life.

It's working. I know it is. And I sense an awakening.

Slowly, painfully slowly, the film clears over Kumugwe's eyes. When I feel I can neither absorb nor release any more water, when every cell in my body feels ready to collapse from fatigue, Kumugwe's pupils constrict and I snap back into myself.

"Whoa!" Nick says, and Kumugwe's right hand twitches.

~ **20**~

NICK LOOKS AT ME with raised eyebrows, drops Kumugwe's arm, and swims around the god's rejuvenated body toward me.

"Father!" Harmony calls to him, swimming to his side, but he's not all here yet.

"Celeste! Are you all right?"

I notice how natural Nick looks in the water. He swims like he was raised in it.

"I'm fine!" When he's within reach, I pull him toward me and feel grounded again, though we're bobbing on the surface of the water.

We watch as what started in Kumugwe's right hand spreads until the twitching encompasses every awakened muscle, raising rippling waves around us.

"You, ah, you kinda disappeared a little bit, like you were, I don't know, coming apart." Nick studies me like he's never seen me before.

"Yes, I did. It's something I learned to do in Kumugwe's castle. Don't worry, though, I can control it." I downplay what just happened. I can't tell him I was starting to feel lost in Kumugwe's brittle body before his cells began to respond.

"This is gonna sound crazy, but while I was holding his arm, I think I could feel your pulse in his body. Is that possible? Because . . . wow!"

"You felt it?" It thrills me to imagine he experienced what I was doing in my transformed state. "Yes! It's possible!" Did the time I spent in Nick's brain somehow connect us more closely on a physical level? Wow, for sure.

Harmony calls to me, interrupting my moment of happiness. "Why won't he talk to me, Celeste? Look in his eyes again and tell him to talk to me! I'll hold them open again for you!" Her words come out in sobs, and this time her song is sonorous. I feel drawn toward her as if pulled by an unseen hand.

"Keep singing, Harmony!" Nick reminds her.

"Give him time!" I say. "He'll wake up soon!"

And then, something mystical happens.

"Whoa! What now?" Nick glances around us and I understand his exclamation. For as far as I can see, and in every direction, the surface of the sea splashes turbulently as underwater life forms of every imaginable type converge on us.

Tentacles rise and fall gracefully as the octopuses arrive, sea lions bark, schools of fluorescent fish turn the water around us into a glowing ring, and the monsters of the sea circle slowly beyond them all.

"That's my cue for getting out of the water," Nick says. "I'm not too keen on us looking like shark bait. Let's go."

I start back toward the island with him, but just as we approach what's left of it, a deep reverberation from the floor of the sea startles us and we watch as it sinks from sight. Its sudden disappearance sucks us underwater and into the void it has created.

Nick grabs my hands and looks at me with confidence and trust as we're pulled below the surface. Together, calmly, steadily, we breathe in the sea, and wait.

Under the surface, we're surrounded by an abundance of life forms thick in the water and expanding in concentric circles around Kumugwe's body, which starts to resurface as the rumbling settles to a stop. He appears to be fully fleshed and the twitching has stopped. The sea creatures are silent and the water is surprisingly calm. They wait too.

When we resurface, I notice the stark line where Old Man Massive meets the sky has raised just a bit higher, and I swim with Nick through the slippery silent bodies until we're back with Harmony.

"Wake him up, Celeste. Please wake him up." Her chin quivers, and I want nothing more than to hug her.

"Come here, child," I address her as I've been addressed most of my life, "and let's wake him together." I release Nick's hand and open my arms to a girl who has experienced hardships beyond even my own. When she's in my arms, I feel a sense of peacefulness permeate my being and I dissolve, just a little, into her—or maybe she dissolves into me.

We communicate as one being, and I feel the word *aninnik* rise to my lips. We whisper the word in unison several times—"*aninnik, aninnik, aninnik*"—and we continue, our combined voice becoming louder with each successive utterance until we believe beyond doubt our final greeting will raise the dead: "ANINNIK, KUMUGWE!"

We break apart, dazed. We're suspended, hovering in the air over Kumugwe's body. Our last exclamation rolls away over the silent sea. No one breathes.

Slowly, as if pulling against an unyielding chain, Kumugwe raises his right hand from the water and the orichalcum inlays on his spear glow golden, softly at first, then brilliantly. His eyelids fly open and he sees us, his brow furrows and confusion flashes across his face, his torso rises from the water as his great tail dips below him and I see the circles of sea life expand out and away from him.

"Father!" Harmony falls from just above him into his arms. He catches her, keeping his eyes on me as I remain hovering beyond reach in the air above him.

"You . . . you . . ." his voice returns to him in raspy gasps, "you brought me back. How? Why? I was nearing the gates of the underworld when I felt a tickle in my veins. Then I heard your voice," he looks at Harmony, "your voices. I do not understand."

"It was Celeste, father, she did it for me."

"But why? Why, after all we did to her?"

"Because her father is returned to her—I felt him when I was one with her—and she is now a daughter again too."

Kumugwe draws his gaze across the surface of his sea and notices his creatures awaiting acknowledgment. Then he sees Nick, bobbing alone in the water in front of him.

"And who is this slim minion? Are you not the very one who came to my realm in a tube not long ago? Where is the smaller child?"

"He's a good boy, father. Nick came alone this time with Celeste to help find you." She breaks into pitiful sobbing while recounting the state in which we found him and how she thought he was gone forever.

He listens patiently.

"I will address my creatures. Their loyalty is unwavering."

Harmony clings to him. I reunite with Nick in the water, and I pull him under with me just as Kumugwe submerges to speak.

"Creatures large and small," Kumugwe announces to the ample gathering, "I have returned."

Nick and I marvel at the kaleidoscope of colors surrounding us. The gentle undulations of the creatures as they listen to their god mesmerize us, and the weight of their presence indicates the solemnity of the occasion.

"These topsiders are to be protected," he gestures toward us, "for they have done me a great service. We must remain vigilant, however, against topsiders with wicked intentions, for they exist as well."

A shadow darkens his expression. Is he remembering Zoya and the scientists? Does he feel responsible for not discovering their presence and their heinous actions sooner?

"You will alert me to those in our realm who wish ill upon us. I thank you for this gathering. That is all. We return to our tasks."

As quickly as they had assembled, the sea life disperses in splashes and swirls and the water is calm once more. The four of us remain underwater looking at one another in awkward silence until Kumugwe asks, "Who did this to me? Who is responsible for my near death?" His questions carry a threat, and I shiver.

I will not betray Old Man Massive, and Nick honestly doesn't know how the intimidating god was trapped on the island.

"Father?" Harmony speaks timidly. "In your anger, you slammed your spear into the sea bottom, do you remember? And do you remember the great surge in every direction, and how you followed me northward?"

Kumugwe remembers. I can tell by his expression. He looks contrite.

"You shook down the mountain, father, and trapped yourself inside."

I couldn't have made up a better explanation for who was to blame. When Kumugwe looks at me with squinted eyes, I can tell he's looking for validation of Harmony's story. I keep my face expressionless, and he finally turns away.

"To you, then, Celeste," his words are filled with hesitation, "I owe . . . what no god has ever owed a mortal."

"You owe me nothing, really. Nothing but my freedom and your promise never to harm the good people topside."

"But that is not enough. I must give you something. I owe you my life." He looks down toward the sea floor, apparently lost in thought, and when he raises his head back to look at me, he's made a decision.

"You will take this." It's not an offer, it's a command. Kumugwe extends his spear toward me in upright open palms. "You returned this treasure to me once, and I am honor-bound to gift it to you. You are the rightful owner now. Use it responsibly, as I have not."

I don't move a muscle.

Nick nudges me. "Take it, Celeste," he whispers bubbles in my ear. They tickle, and I laugh, breaking the tension I feel in every fiber of my body.

Kumugwe's expression remains somber. He's waiting for me to take the spear from his hands, hands that mere moments ago were incapable of holding anything.

"Take it, Celeste," Harmony tells me. "And what you wish for it to be, it will be when it's yours."

The spear draws me to it as if it knows I'm to take it.

"Do I need to decide right away what I wish it to be?" I ask. The responsibility of owning such an object is too great for me at this moment.

"It will wait," Kumugwe assures me. "It will know when you are ready."

Yes, but will I know? I take the spear from Kumugwe's hands and am surprised once more by how light it feels. For a moment I fear a flashback of sorrow, but it doesn't happen. Instead, I feel exhilarated and, as if expressing my inner joy, the orichalcum pattern on the spear, my spear, glows a golden-green.

My mystical moment doesn't last long. Odin's ravens dive-bomb the water just above our heads.

"Ah! My troublesome brother." Kumugwe chuckles when he recognizes the birds. "Still confined in my castle! He will not be happy with me. He should have stayed home." Without another word, he and Harmony swim southward.

When I consider what became of Kumugwe while he was trapped outside his realm, I shudder when I imagine what we'll find inside the prison of his collapsed underwater castle.

"Let's go," I say, grabbing Nick's hand with my free hand. I point my spear forward and we follow in Kumugwe's swift wake effortlessly.

Will Odin be alive when we get there?

~ 21 ~

BEFORE WE REACH the castle, Harmony breaks from Kumugwe's side in a bizarre, staggering motion and screams.

"No! Not now! They can't do this to me! Don't let them do this to me!" She continues to lurch unnaturally, and Kumugwe looks at her as if witnessing a new life form—with awe, fascination, and a touch of horror.

"What has possessed you, child of my heart?" Kumugwe wraps his arms around her to contain her movements and looks to me as if I know the answer. "Fix her, girl! Fix my child!"

"But I don't know what's wrong! Harmony, talk to me. Who are *they*, and what are they doing to you?"

"My birth parents planted a chip in me somewhere like the chips they're putting in their creature army! Lilith has a control, I saw it when we were in the cave putting the skeletons into the squishy bodies, and when she moved a button on it, my arms and legs moved in ways I didn't want them to move! Look! I can't stop!" Her limbs struggle against Kumugwe's unbreakable embrace. "They must be testing the monsters!"

Harmony stops lurching for a moment and we all wait to see if she'll start again. We let her words sink in.

"This chip, my child, what does it look like, and where is it within you?" Kumugwe releases her and turns her slowly, looking for where such a chip might be.

"I snatched one from inside one of the blobs before leaving the underwater cavern laboratory and I put it in a pocket, but I lost it. It was made of metal, a tiny thing, no bigger than Celeste's smallest fingernail. It must have washed away in the giant wave we swam in before you were trapped, father. I don't know where it is, but I want it out of me!"

Harmony looks at me. They all look at me.

"You brought me back to life, mysterious girl. Surely you can find this small chip." Kumugwe raises his eyebrows, juts out his lower lip, and looks at me with a boyish expression of hopefulness.

"And you helped save me too, Celeste," Nick says. "If you do that falling apart thing and look into Harmony's eyes, maybe you'll be able to see where the chip is and, I don't know, get it out or break it or something."

A smack of spectacularly intricate jellyfish swirls around us, their tendrils trailing behind gracefully, their bodies emitting flashes of brilliant light in colors rivaling the nacreous clouds in Odin's realm, and they give me an idea.

"Harmony, I've seen you change your body several times. Can you make yourself transparent? I know it sounds crazy, but maybe we could see inside you if you could. Kind of like those jellyfish?"

She looks at the jellyfish and reaches her hand out to touch one as it passes. It wriggles around her arm and when she giggles, I feel the tickle. It flashes and leaves her, joining the swarm of others on their way to who-knows-where.

"I don't think I can, Celeste. I can be part fish—like now, when I need a tail to swim faster—but I'm mostly human. And jellyfish aren't really fish, you know. But I'll try." Harmony closes her eyes and we all watch, anticipating that at any moment, Harmony will become see-through. But she doesn't.

She opens her eyes and looks down at her body. "I tried, really I did. Will you look through my eyes and find the chip, Celeste? Because I can't stand it, knowing they can make me do something I don't want to do."

"Do this for us," Kumugwe says, "and I will gift you with more treasures than you can imagine."

I really just want to get to his castle, find Odin alive, and go back to the village. But I can tell we're not going anywhere until I at least try to find the chip.

"I can't promise I'll find it, but I'll try." I swim to Harmony and face her, holding her hands. "Keep your eyes open, Harmony, and let's see what I can do."

When I look into her eyes I feel the tingle start at the back of my head and I let it move through my body until I feel myself start to disperse. I'm in her eyes, through her eyes, and into her head. I don't have to go too far before I find it, and I'm worried. The chip is completely encased in and fused fast to the cells of her brainstem. There's no way I could remove or disable it—even if I knew much about it— without potentially damaging her brain in ways I can't imagine. I can't do it. I won't.

I back out of her, I tell her without words to blink, and when she does, I snap back into myself. How will I explain what I've seen?

"Did you find it? Is it gone?" Harmony reaches for her head, but before she can touch it, she twitches again and her tail transforms to legs that try to march her through the water. "Oh! Celeste! Why didn't you take it out? Please make it stop!"

If it weren't so tragic, what she's doing would appear comical. It's really not funny at all, and I feel horrible for having failed her.

I need a good reason for why I didn't take it out, a reason that won't scare her any more than she already is. In time I'll learn how to remove it without causing damage—or Ryder might know how to do it already. Or we just wait until we stop the scientists. Then it won't be an issue.

"I found it, yes, but I had a really good idea while I was in there. Let's think about this. Maybe it's actually a good thing you have this chip in you."

Nick frowns. "But it can't be good if they're doing what you say they're doing—making an army to control more survivors."

"Right, but since Harmony has the chip, we'll be able to track their progress! See? And Harmony will be able to tell us—we'll be able to see—what they're making her do, so we'll know how, and when, to defend ourselves."

I feel pretty smug about my cover-up, but Harmony doesn't look too happy, even though she's stopped lurching. Kumugwe isn't convinced either. Nick gets it, though, and backs me up.

"Okay, I see your point, but what if they make her do something bad to us?" He moves a little farther away from her in the water, and she looks offended.

"But I promise never to hurt you or Celeste again. I'd never mean to, anyway."

Nick doesn't appear to be convinced, and I have my own reasons for not trusting her childlike motivations.

"And really, my birth parents probably don't even remember they put a chip in me. I only discovered it in the cavern, and Lilith—the woman I'll never call mother—didn't see me move when she played with the controls and made the blobs jiggle. They left me in the water when they tore away from Zoya without even knowing how long I could hold my breath. They probably think I'm dead." She swims to Kumugwe for comfort. He cradles her like a baby.

She has no love for her birth parents. I just need to convince her to protect the rest of us from them. "Harmony, can you see how you might be able to help us against those mean people?" I hope she can see how.

She looks up at Kumugwe's fretful face before turning back to me. "But that would mean I'd have to come back with you when you return topside, right? I'd have to be a girl like you, and you'd have to protect me and make sure I don't hurt any nice people."

She's smarter than I give her credit for being. "You're right. And you'd be doing a good and noble thing for the survivors who are good people and who are struggling to rebuild their world. And when the time comes, I'll remove the chip."

When the time comes. Time never comes, it just goes.

Harmony appears to consider what I said.

"You owe the topsiders nothing, my little music-maker." Kumugwe cradles her more tightly.

"But I owe Celeste something. I nearly killed her, father." She leaves the protection of his arms, transforms back into her tail, and swims over to me. She takes my hands in hers and says, "I'll do as you ask."

"Let's get to the castle fast, then," I say, "and release Odin and stop those cruel people."

"I sure hope you know what you're doing, Pipsqueak," Nick mumbles.

I don't answer.

~ 22 ~

OUR JOURNEY to the castle is slowed by Harmony's fits of movement, which frequently force her legs from her tail. The transformation looks painful, but she tells us it's not. For the most part, her actions appear uncoordinated—until she does something that makes us all gasp.

She thrusts her right arm over her head and forward as if throwing a ball, and at the peak of the throw, what appears to be a long, sharp metal object springs from her hand. For a moment, she's wielding a sword, and in the next instant, the threatening weapon retracts and is gone.

"Oh, no!" Harmony looks horrified. "How did they do that? How did that thing come out of me? And I heard something too!"

We all back away from her, even Kumugwe, who appears more troubled than ever.

"You heard something? What?" I chastise myself for not exploring more while I was dissolved in her. Why didn't I see anything beyond the chip?

"Voices. Lilith's, and Thurston's—he's my birth father. They sound happy—well, she does—but I can't understand what they're saying. And other voices." Harmony squeezes her eyes closed. "My sister's, I think, but she sounds like a little girl. Isn't she your age? And Blanche. She's there too. Oh! And a boy is crying. He sounds so sad." She opens her eyes. "It stopped. I don't hear anything."

We all have our mouths wide open and I cough when a curious little clownfish explores the space between my jaws.

"How are you hearing them," I ask, but I know it's because of the chip.

"The sound is far away, but it's far away inside my head. How did they make a weapon come from my hand?"

"Yeah," Nick says, "never mind about the voices. If she can't stop them from turning her body into a weapon—"

"But she can, right, Harmony?" I want her to say, *"Sure I can. Piece of cake,"* but I have my doubts.

"I . . . I don't know. It just happened so fast I couldn't stop it." She clasps her hands behind her back and looks to Kumugwe, presumably for reassurance, but his mouth is still hanging open, filled with tiny fluorescent fish that have mistaken it for a safe space in the vast sea. For a moment, I'm mesmerized by the blue-green glow behind his teeth.

When Kumugwe neither speaks nor moves toward her, I ask, "Did you feel anything, any kind of sign that something was going to happen? Because if there's even a hint or a twitch or a suspicion, even if you can't control what's about to happen, you could warn us. You could turn away, or resist it."

If I'd been in front of her when her arm became a sword, I could have been sliced in half.

"NOW!" she screams, and both arms become weapons.

"Abomination!" Kumugwe spews out a school of neons, which tumble through the water in every direction before righting themselves and swimming off. "Not you, my child, but what they have done to you." He makes a gesture of opening his arms to her, but hesitates, withdrawing the offer.

I question my decision to leave the chip in her brain, but I had to. At least until we know more. And with this troubling new development, will we ever make it to Kumugwe's castle?

"I did it, Celeste, I warned you, right?" She looks horrified as the swords spring in and out of her hands several times before stopping.

"Yes! You did. Thank you!" I have to be careful with my next proposal. "This must scare you, Harmony. Until we can find out what their plans are, you're going to have to keep your distance from everyone. Do you see why?"

"Of course I see why. How could I not see why? But I don't think I want to do this anymore."

She can't change her mind now, especially if she's hearing conversations. Did I overlook something while I was in her brain? It's possible, but what if there's only the one chip?

"Let me go back in, Harmony. There might be something I can do without removing the chip."

"No!" Nick protests. "It's too dangerous! You saw what she can do. You shouldn't get anywhere near her." He positions himself between the two of us, and I instinctively reach out and pull him farther away from her. If her hands become swords again, she'll cut him.

"Silence, boy!" Kumugwe's voice booms through the water. "She will go back in and stop this horror."

"Hey!" he shouts back at Kumugwe and I'm terrified the water god will take away Nick's ability to breathe here. He doesn't, though. Instead, he looks amused. "You don't make decisions for her, understand? She'll decide for herself!" Nick looks at me, his dazzling eyes blazing, and I want to kiss him.

But this isn't the place or time for that.

"Maybe there's another way. I'll try it from here," I tell them. Several slippery-looking eels swim through the space between Harmony and me. They look scary, but they're harmless. I hand my spear to Nick and he takes it from me hesitantly. Kumugwe crosses his arms and watches us, his expression somber.

"You don't have to do this," Nick whispers. "You don't have to rescue everyone."

"But look at her! She's petrified. If I can help her, I have to. It won't take long to find out if I can."

With his free hand he brushes back my drifting hair, rests his hand on the back of my neck and draws me close to him. He touches his forehead to mine. "You're a better person than me," he says.

"No, I'm not," I whisper, strengthened by his warmth. I press my cheek against his before turning toward Harmony.

"Keep your eyes open, Harmony, and look at me until I tell you to blink, okay?"

"Okay. But I don't want to hurt you, so be careful."

If I were careful, I wouldn't be here.

I stare into her eyes over a distance of salty water until the tingling begins. I feel my glow and know I'm dissolving. I allow myself to be drawn into and through her eyes. I see the chip again, and it still looks too dangerous to touch.

Spreading out farther, I notice tiny reflective specks scattered throughout the muscles in her arms and legs. I don't know whether these are due to her ability to transform and camouflage herself or if they're the mechanisms the scientists are using to control her. I wrap particles of myself around all of the specks in her right arm and I communicate with Harmony.

Do you feel anything different in this arm?

Yes. What's happening? I don't want to hurt you.

You can't hurt me in here. I sure hope this is true. *Try to camouflage your right arm. Tell me if you can.*

I wait.

Yes. I can change its color. What does it mean?

It means I've found the culprits, the things turning your body into weapons.

Can you make them go away?

This is a task I've never performed. I've absorbed water from Nick's brain while staying in my own body, and I've rehydrated Kumugwe's cells while in my dissolved state. Can I absorb all of these flickering foreign objects in Harmony's muscles and take them with me without injuring myself, or her? It's a risk I have to take if I want to keep the others safe when they're around her.

Yes. I'll need a little more time to locate them all. Be patient, and keep your eyes open.

I spread myself throughout her body, wrapping each speck I find in multiple particles of myself. It makes me feel itchy. I don't like it. There are so many, and I'm wrapped around them all. Time to take them with me.

Okay, I'm leaving now, I tell Harmony.

It hurts, Celeste! Why does it hurt?

It hurts me too, but I'm almost out. Ready? Blink.

She blinks, and I don't know if the cry of pain is from her or from me. I feel as if I've been stabbed all over by tiny blades.

"You're bleeding!" Nick tells me, rushing to my side.

I look down to see tiny rivulets of purple blood seep from my pores and dissipate into a passing sea current. I feel an overwhelming urge to cough, but I'm afraid to. When I can't suppress it any longer, pain rips through me, I clutch my stomach, my body spasms, and from my mouth pours all of the tiny metal pieces I've absorbed. The bleeding stops, and soon the pain stops too.

Nick returns my spear and waves his hands in the water, pushing the pieces away from us. "Celeste! Are you okay? You shouldn't do that again—disappearing and going inside people—it's not safe!" He wraps his arms around me and then whispers, "When you were in there, Harmony's whole body glowed. And she started to look like you."

He doesn't want to lose me again. We cling to one another and I think about what he said. Something feels wrong, though.

"I'm okay, really," I say before letting him go. "Harmony? You're safe now. The master chip is still in there, but you won't be throwing swords anymore. Maybe you'll just be able to share what you hear now. Harmony?"

She turns her head toward me and I gasp. "I can't see," she whispers.

~ 23 ~

"WHAT HAVE YOU DONE?" Kumugwe booms. He doesn't hesitate this time, but swims to Harmony and cradles her in his arms again. "Look at me, child! Let me see your eyes."

Nick tries to hold me back. Instead, I pull him with me, and I'm horrified to see what Kumugwe sees. Harmony's eyes appear to have been . . . shredded.

"The pieces of metal," I blurt, "those things," I point to the flickering objects floating in the water around us, "they were all throughout her body. I had to get them out! Harmony, I'm sorry! I'm so, so sorry!"

Kumugwe brushes me away with the back of his hand, and Nick and I tumble through the water. The current created by his brush-off sends us careening far from them.

I guess he's forgotten I just saved his life, but I've known all along how little he cares for topsiders—other than for Harmony.

"This is crazy," Nick says when we stop spinning. "We have to get out of here. They're both dangerous."

He's right, but I can't leave things like this.

"Celeste!" Harmony calls to me, her head scanning right and left though she sees nothing. "It'll be okay. Father has eyes he'll give me—isn't that right, father?—and you'll repair my vision. I'm not afraid."

Nick and I swim back toward them, and Kumugwe holds Harmony protectively.

"This is true," he says, looking at me with caution. "You have seen them, have you not?"

I nod. How could I ever forget his gigantic vat of eyeballs? I wish Nick and I were back in the village again making our friends laugh and squirm with eyeball stories. Now they don't seem as funny.

"We will select the finest eyes and you will see again. And how is my daughter feeling otherwise?" He lifts each of her arms gently, one at a time, but keeps her hands pointed away from him.

"I feel . . . safe. I heard murmurs of bedtime from the voices far away—the poor boy is still whimpering—so perhaps I won't know until the topsiders wake if my body is my own again. Celeste? Are you there?"

"I'm here," I say, and Kumugwe allows me to touch her hand.

"I think you've stopped them from making me move. I didn't know about the other parts they added to their beasts, I worried only about the chip. What did you do with the pieces of metal? Maybe we can figure out how they work."

I feel foolish I didn't think of holding on to some of them, and when I turn around, Nick is already swimming after a few of the tiny pieces sinking in the deep water below us.

When I think of all he's done for me, all the times he's put himself in danger for me, I'm filled with guilt over this latest predicament. It's time to get out of here.

"Nick has them in a pocket," I tell her. "I'm sorry I hurt you," I say again, and she shakes her head slowly.

"Don't be sorry. Now we know more, and we'll stop them from hurting others. Are we almost home, father?"

~ 113 ~

"Very near. Let us make haste and end this most troubling journey." Kumugwe turns on his tail and, carrying Harmony in his arms, swims away.

I hold my spear in my right hand, Nick takes my other, and we follow them. Kumugwe is right, we're closer than I thought, and soon the castle rises from the ocean floor before us. I'm shocked to find it's not a wreck of collapsed rocks.

"Whoa," Nick whispers as we approach the main door, "this is unbelievable."

I agree, and I feel a sinking in my stomach when I anticipate what we're about to find inside the castle.

Kumugwe waves a hand and the door opens. We follow him inside, and much to my surprise, everything is exactly as I remember it, including the vat of eyeballs near the door.

"You have done well, caretakers of my castle." Kumugwe addresses the pillars of sea lions holding up the ceilings and they bark softly. He turns to me. "You look surprised, girl. Did you think my creatures would leave my castle in ruins while I've been away?"

I don't know how to answer, so I say nothing, but I'm sure he can read the amazement in my expression.

"They have rebuilt our home countless times after myriad shifts in the planet have caused it to crumble. They are masters of their craft. To my infuriating brother!" He sets Harmony upon a seashell seat and strokes her long pink hair before traveling to the room at the end of the hall.

I hold my breath and squeeze Nick's hand while Kumugwe fiddles with a lock, and then I hear him.

"Celeste? Is that you? Have you returned to me at last?"

Coming from an old god who sounds like he's gasping his final breaths, his words make me sad. I release Nick's hand, wrap his fingers around my spear, and dash down the hall just as Kumugwe opens the door. I push my way around him and am the first one to look into Odin's eyes.

I do my best to hide my astonishment at his condition, but I don't fool him.

"Not a pretty sight, eh?" he says.

As shriveled and dehydrated as Kumugwe was when we found him on the dry island, Odin appears to have swallowed a small sea. His distended flesh undulates around him, nearly filling the room in which he's been imprisoned.

I cannot imagine—don't want to imagine—what it will take to bring him back to his normal size and shape. I don't even know how we'll get him out of the room.

And then he laughs, and when he laughs, I bob up and down in the waves he creates, and his laughter is contagious, even though I really want to cry.

I can't help it. I giggle at the ridiculous sight before me—the bloated, laughing blob of a god and the predicament he's in—and then I can't stop. I laugh and laugh and then Kumugwe joins in, and I see Nick peering over Kumugwe's shoulder and the expression on his face makes me laugh even harder, and Nick's horrified expression changes to laughter—a panicky kind of laughter but laughter nonetheless—and then I hear Harmony giggling in her seashell seat in the main room and it's all just too much for me and I have to leave, I have to leave this horrible room, this oppressive castle, this place where both of these gods tried to keep me from leaving, tried to keep me for their own selfish purposes without asking what I might want, what I might need in order to be happy, and I feel like I might burst apart, like I might explode and tear the castle apart again, but I can't hurt Nick and so I squeeze my eyes closed really hard and try not to see the insanity of everything around me—try not to see the vat of eyeballs I'm supposed to repair Harmony's eyesight with—but I still see it, I see it all, and the visions are ghastly and I want to go home, I want to go home to where my father waits for me with fear I'll never return, and he might be right but NO!

"STOP IT! STOP IT EVERYONE! SHUT UP! JUST SHUT UP!" I push my way through the prison door past Kumugwe and Nick out the main door and I scream and scream and scream into the boundless sea.

~ **24** ~

MY SCREAMS ATTRACT the attention of crustaceans I recall from a dream long ago. Several shiny black hermit crab-like creatures scuttle up to me and stop, their eye stocks wriggling about, their antennae reaching out to touch my legs. They tickle.

Should I be frightened? In my dream, their large claws opened to swallow people from a shoreline. But these little guys look harmless, and they stop me from screaming. Pretty sure they delivered my father to the beach near our village too.

It's strange, but I feel like they're waiting for something. I reach down to touch them, but they retreat into their shells in a snap, like tightly drawn window shades being released.

I turn back to take Nick away from the disaster in the castle—how could I have left him in there?—and I swim right into him. He has my spear in one hand and Harmony's hand in his other. He returns the spear to me.

"We need to go. Now." His voice is subdued, but adamant. Laughter continues inside, though not as uproarious as before.

"Yes, let's go, Celeste." Harmony holds her free hand in front of her, for protection maybe, or in search of me. "We should leave before he changes his mind."

"Before *who* changes his mind?"

"My father. I told him I'm bound to help you. I want to help you."

"I'm ready," I say, taking her outstretched hand and trying not to look into the vacant pits where her eyes once were. This was my fault. I should have considered what all those metal objects might do when I removed them from her body.

"I told him I'll return when I know those people won't be able to crack open the planet again."

"What?" Nick looks at Harmony and then turns away abruptly. We're both having a hard time looking at her face without eyes. "Your parents were the ones who caused all the destruction? Did they make the ooze too? And how? How'd they do it?"

I scrunch my eyebrows at him. It sounds like he's accusing Harmony too.

"They're *not* my parents." Harmony pouts and pulls her hand away from Nick. But I hold on, and in a startling flash, I experience her parents' betrayal.

I cling, I whimper, my tiny arms and legs flail spasmodically when I'm tossed through the air, and when I hit the water, its coldness catches my breath away. A man groans and a woman cackles. I sink, still holding my breath, eyes stinging with the salt water, until I'm pulled by something unseen below me.

I'm cradled in gigantic arms by a creature who looks at me quizzically and reminds me to breathe.

But it's not me. It's Harmony.

"Oh!" I gasp, and pull her to me.

"It's okay," she tells me. "Sorry, Nick. Your questions just make me remember, and it hurts."

"No, I'm sorry. I shouldn't have snapped at you like that. It wasn't your fault."

Her shared vision gives me an idea. "Harmony, could you make him see—make me see too—what you witnessed in the submarine?"

"I think so," she says, searching for Nick's hand.

As soon as we're all linked, Nick and I are in Harmony's mind, inside the submarine. Switches, dials, and long, metal probes line the walls. Diagrams and charts litter the countertops and hang from walls, but we can't make sense of them.

We see Blanche and a young Sharon discuss the charts, talking about things like lasers and changing ionic composition, and there's an unpleasantly lingering stale, sterile odor.

Harmony releases us from her memory. "Their experiments shook the planet till it cracked open—I know that—and the ooze came out of one of the openings near Zoya."

Nick's eyes question mine, and I explain what little I know about the tortured octopus through my brief interactions with her in my dreams and when I found her in the ooze.

"Then, why didn't Kumugwe stop them?" Nick's question plagues me. "He's the god down here. Wouldn't he have known about what they were doing to his waters and with the octopus?"

"Her name was Zoya," Harmony says. Her defenses are up again. "And you said you were ready to go. I guess I should just stay here and let you figure out how to save your own land topside. Maybe my father's right, and I shouldn't be helping—"

"Please, Harmony!" I cut her off. "Please keep your word to me!"

The laughter has stopped in the castle, and a feeling of doom shivers my blood when I can't think of a way we all might escape if Kumugwe changes his mind about us. Even if we were able to swim fast enough to get to the surface, Odin's ravens are sure to be circling, waiting for me to bring their god back to his domain.

And we need Harmony.

"If you can hear those people through the chip they planted in you, then you can be a part of stopping them. You can finally get your revenge against them for what they did to you." I have no idea what her revenge would look like. "And it's not just topside they're threatening. Any damage they do to our land will affect the seas too. You know this."

Her pout remains. "Yes. I know this. I'll keep my word. I'll come with you, and we'll stop them."

Nick's questions haunt me again, though. The caretakers at the children's home taught us the gods were all-powerful and omniscient in their realms. If that were true, then why couldn't Kumugwe have found them, stopped them, and protected Zoya—one of his gentlest creatures?

"Nick, the seas are enormous. There's no way Kumugwe can know about every creature in every cave and underwater tunnel around the planet."

But the damage to the planet had shaken everything, including the sea, and poisoned most of its surface with the vile ooze. How could he not have known?

"I guess you're right. I just thought . . . you know."

"I know," I say. We're both wondering the same thing.

When the villagers chanted to Odin for rain, didn't he know they'd die without it? Yet he withheld it from them. He taught me how to make rain while trying to convince me to stay with him, to help him, but from what I remember, his one-eyed vision was narrow. He relied on his ravens to bring him information—ravens waiting for him even now.

Why do they wait? Why not fly away and live their lives independent from him? And didn't Odin tell me he'd die if everyone stopped believing in him? Why, then, did he withhold rain for so long? A dead population can't keep a god alive.

Maybe we've been fooled all along into believing the planet and its inhabitants need the gods. Seems to me it's the other way around.

I feel like I might throw up, but there's nothing in my stomach. Everything feels like it's caving in on me, like the pressure of the sea is threatening to crush me.

I thought I'd be freeing Odin from his prison room, but I'm done with saving the gods. I could do it, I'm sure. I could reverse the action I took when I rehydrated Kumugwe, but what then? More childish, selfish games? I'm done with being a pawn in their games.

Kumugwe will have to find a way to release his brother from the confining space. They seem to be on good terms again, and it's clear to me now they've been quarreling off and on for eons. Maybe Odin will float to the surface and evaporate his excess fluid once he's touched by the sun again.

I don't know. I don't care anymore.

And maybe he needs to return to Asgard to keep the planet in balance, but maybe he doesn't. Maybe it would be better for all of civilization if the gods just stayed out of our lives.

What a fool I've been, leaving my people, leaving my father so I could rescue the gods. Rescue the gods! Me, a pipsqueak with crazy powers! And putting Nick in danger yet again. What was I thinking?

The gods should have been working to rescue us, but they weren't. They're only interested in themselves. What have I done?

Maybe it's time for the gods to die.

~ **25** ~

"**CELESTE? LET'S GO.** You look a little green, and not the nice glowy green. You're not going back in there, are you?" Nick looks as uneasy as I feel.

"No! No. They can take care of themselves, right, Harmony? After all, they are gods." I don't even try to hide my sarcasm.

"Yes, they'll be fine. They've been in worse situations before you showed up, and they're always trying to outdo one another. It ends with laughter, and then they go back to their own routines."

I'm such a fool. So these are just games to them. But I'm not sure how Kumugwe would have made it back to his castle and his routine without my involvement. Old Man Massive might have finally let him go. He could have rehydrated on his own with enough time back in his element.

The gods have been playing games with one another—and with innocent mortals. It makes my stomach turn again. But we should be on our way to the surface instead of sharing memories.

What's the fastest way? What's the safest way?

Harmony senses my distress—she must feel what I feel whether we're connected by thought or touch—and she hums a tiny snippet of a tune. It sounds like a request to me, but it's just a song. I need to remember what her songs can do, though. I need to remember how she lured me over the stinking water into her sandcastle a lifetime ago. Do I block my ears?

"Celeste, don't be silly," Harmony says, and although I want to pretend I don't know what she's talking about, I do. "I'm just giving them instructions."

"What's she talking about, Celeste? Harmony, what are you talking about?"

I hear creaky, scratchy little noises behind me, where the hermit crabs are still standing. They're the "them" she's talking about. She's giving them instructions. This is what they've been waiting for.

"You know. Instructions. Now, don't either of you question me. Just close your eyes," she tells me and Nick.

She can't see us, so she must sense our hesitation, must know Nick and I are looking into one another's eyes, both of us on the edge of panic, both of us questioning the other with some dread in our hearts.

She can't see. How does closing our eyes make any sense?

"If you want to go home before my father changes his mind, that is. Do it now." Harmony tilts her head, waiting for an indication of our compliance.

"Okay," I say. Nick and I nod at the same time and close our eyes, though it feels contrary to what I should be doing—finding a fast way home—and the next thing I know, I'm careening through the water in a slick, glowing tube. Nick and Harmony keep pace with me in tubes on either side, and when I look behind me, I swear I can see a shiny black hermit crab at the far end of my spectacular tunnel.

We pass over deep coral reefs and sunken mountaintops and through schools of fluorescent fish and pods of dolphins and lumbering manatees, but as breathtaking as the speed and sights are, I'm still afraid we could be captured. And I don't trust Harmony. Why would she have left Kumugwe, the only being—besides me, occasionally—who cares about her?

She's smiling. She turns toward me, and in a horrifying vision I imagine her ripping through her tube and tearing into mine, stopping me before I reach my destination—wherever these tubes are taking us—and laughing at my trust in her, laughing with her torn eye sockets quivering in the water, laughing at the power I believe I have to stop her birth parents from destroying what remains of a planet they've already torn apart.

And I envision her waving a hand at Nick again, taking away his ability to breathe in this unforgiving environment—killing him.

Stop it, I tell myself. Calm down. She could have done all of this back at the castle if she'd wanted to.

A twinge of doubt lingers, though.

I turn away from her and look at Nick. He raises his eyebrows in a way that says, "What's the matter?" Can he see lingering remnants of that terrifying vision in my face? I do my best to smile, but just as Odin could read my expression when I saw what had become of him, Nick can tell my smile's not real. And I can tell he'll do anything, everything, to keep me safe. This is what brings a genuine smile to my lips.

Just as he returns my smile, I feel myself tossed into the air, the dry, sun-soaked air, and I land on my behind with a dull thump in a soft mound of sand. Two more thumps and Nick and Harmony land on either side of me. Harmony is back in her legs.

I remember this beach. I see an enormous span of wall on the hillside where I threw this spear, my spear, into the silvery-pink water, and watched as it turned to turquoise. I point to the wall, a question in my eyes.

"Bridger built it," Nick says. "Stopped a tidal wave. Oh, and Katie froze the wave before it hit, so I guess she's to thank too. I keep forgetting you weren't here then. It's a long, long way around, but you could fly us over it faster."

I remember plucking Bridger from the apple tree and the sorrow he expressed when his first little boat couldn't save any lives. I'm not the only one feeling responsible for the fate of others, then. It's a humbling thought.

Harmony holds up a hand. "Shhh! Lilith and Thurston are talking again. It's echoey, but it sounds like they're saying they're not ready yet. They're pleased with their progress. They started talking while we were in the tunnels, but the travel noise made it hard to hear."

"Yeah, about those tunnels," I say. "What exactly are they?"

"Those water tunnels," Nick says, "are how Chimney and I found you. Well, they brought us to you. I don't know how. Don't you remember being in one? When I, you know, woke you up?" His copper cheeks glow. Pretty sure he's blushing. I know I am.

"The hermit crabs are my friends," Harmony giggles. She bows her head and plays with the sand, picking up handfuls and letting it sift between her fingers. She looks so innocent. "I called to them before leaving the castle with Nick, and they waited for us. They spin the water tunnels from inside their shells and grab you with their claws. I told you to close your eyes so you wouldn't be afraid."

Just like in my dream. Hermit crabs with special powers.

But something doesn't make sense to me. "Then, why were you in such a hurry to leave if you knew Kumugwe would just let you come with us?"

"I already told you. He could've changed his mind. He doesn't really understand why I want to help topsiders, especially since they were the ones who threw me away."

"Why *do* you want to help us?" Nick asks.

"Isn't revenge for what they did to me a good enough reason? But no. I should thank them for tossing me into the water to a father who loves me and a home that's more beautiful than anything I've seen topside. I'm helping because Lilith and Thurston broke the sea floor. They tortured a loving creature and they poisoned our home. I can't let them do that again. They have to be stopped before I can return to my father." She stops playing with the sand. She's about to cry.

Can a person with shattered eyes cry?

Even though I feel her torment, she frightens me.

It's time to return to the village. Do I bring her there looking as she does? I see the expression on Nick's face when he looks at her. The young ones have endured so much, but this is horrifying.

"Harmony? Would you let me protect your eyes so when you're ready for new ones, the area will be clean? There's so much sand and dust and—"

"Of course."

She bows her head again and allows me to tie my emerald scarf around her head, over the empty places.

~ **26** ~

I PULL HARMONY to her feet and keep hold of one hand. In my other hand is the spear. Were the sacrifices I've made and the danger I've put my friends in worth it for this metal inlaid stick of wood, this thing I'll need to keep safe so it won't fall into the wrong hands again, as it did with Sharon? I'd be a fool to think so, but I've been wrong before.

"It's waiting, you know," Harmony says.

"What's waiting? Where?" I glance around the beach for lurking dangers and shiny black hermit crabs, but there's nothing more than sand and water and darkening sky, and Bridger's great wall on the distant hill.

"Your spear. It's waiting for you to give it a purpose."

Is my mind really that open to her? She smiles, and I shiver a little.

"You should give it a name," Nick suggests. "Something impressive. Something powerful." It looks like he's searching for just the right name.

"Maybe we should get to the village and see how our friends are coming along with their plans first," I say. Unless Harmony is lying about the scientists' readiness, there will be time for naming and purposing my spear later.

"Yeah, you're right." He gazes over the land between the water and the wall. "Should we walk to the wall? Hard to believe this was all cracked open or covered in ooze not long ago."

"Was it really not long ago?" That's what I find hard to believe. I remember all the horrifying things that happened here—the pursuit of Sharon in her vulture form, the terrifying rescue of Thunder and Chimney and Orville from the fissures, Orville's excruciating fight for his life and asking me to return him to the stinking waters—and here I stand, holding the spear I mistakenly thought had ended all the troubles for the survivors of The Event.

"Well, it did seem like forever while you were gone." He shakes water from his sea-swept hair and takes my hand and Harmony's. We start walking toward the wall.

When we get back to the village, there won't be time for breezy walks on the beach.

I have a nagging feeling I should've already learned more about the scientists, but how could I have when even Sharon didn't seem to know they were alive after they abandoned her? How could any of us have known what they were working on? And what *are* they working on, what's the purpose of their creature army? They can't be planning to destroy the planet—they wouldn't be able to do that without ensuring their own deaths—but what, then?

I blame the gods. They should've known about these people. And maybe they did. Odin showed me the ooze returning to the sea during the time of fluxes. Did he know about the scientists' cruel laboratory deep underwater? Wouldn't he have told his quarrelsome brother about it?

Was it just another game to them, watching how mortals react to devastation? And here we are, on our own with nothing more than our powers. Powers we may or may not be able to keep. Who knows how long they'll last if Lilith and

Thurston can still cause ionic fluctuations from their new laboratory?

Nick looks exhausted—not sure why I'm not—and I'm eager to see my father and my friends. Enough trudging through shifting sand. I stop, and Nick raises his eyebrows. I smile, and he smiles back.

"If you don't mind, let's fly." I wrap one arm around Harmony and guide her arm around my waist. Nick already knows how to hold onto me. How I wish it were just the two of us right here, alone on this beach. I look at him before taking flight and read the same wish in his eyes.

"I'm ready," Harmony says, interrupting this beautiful moment. And she's still wearing that smile. It's hard to read a smile when there are no eyes to interpret it.

Part of me wants to leave her here, abandon her on this beach, pluck my scarf away from her and send her back to Kumugwe. Do we really need to hear what's happening in the laboratory? We know it's not good. We know Bridger is there—frightened and unhappy—with Sharon and Blanche too. We know the monsters will have weaponized limbs and will do as they're directed.

And can we even trust Harmony to tell us the truth?

She could have killed us back in the castle, but she didn't. She let me inside her, allowed me to remove the weaponized particles, leaving her sightless. The connection we have remains a mystery, but I can't deny it.

And I can't abandon her. I have to remember she's a child who just wanted someone to play with.

Kumugwe wanted—wants—to protect her and keep her happy.

And Odin is an ancient god, looking for a companion.

What a world.

"Are we flying yet?"

She may be blind, but she knows we're not flying yet. Nick squeezes me gently and nods, and I lift them both from the ground. It doesn't take long before we're over the village.

Ranger is the first to spot us from where he roams the perimeter, and he comes running as we land. He sniffs Harmony's feet and she giggles. She reaches out her hands toward him, and he sniffs them too, but backs away before she can touch him. I see him looking at my scarf. He lets Nick pet him, and when I kneel down, he delivers a wee welcome lick under my chin.

"This is the child who walked from the sea," Ranger says. "She left the village with the bad sister after you disappeared. I do not understand. Why is she here?"

He lets me hug him—I'm so happy to feel his full, soft coat again—and I see others coming our way when they notice us. "She's here to help us," I say. "Let's meet with Orville and the rest and I'll tell you what we've learned. It's good to be back, Ranger. How's Penelope?"

"You remembered her name." He seems pleased. "She is strong. She will help as well."

"Celeste!" My father calls from down the road and comes running. I meet him halfway, and enveloped in his hug, I feel safe again, safe enough to cry. "Oh! Don't cry, Little Bear. You're home now"—*Home*, he says!—"and everything's going to be all right." He holds me tightly until I stop crying. "Who's the blindfolded girl? Isn't that the scarf we gave you when—"

"Her name is Harmony, and she's the daughter of Kumugwe. Her birth parents are the scientists we need to stop. They're the ones who took you away from me, who took Mom away from me."

More tears. What is it about my father that makes it okay to just be me again? I pull myself together. I can't keep letting The Event—and my family's drop into the fissure that day—haunt me. I still don't know how my father survived the plunge that cracked our home and swallowed everything—but Mom and my puppy didn't survive. I'll probably never know.

At least I have him. There are no other fathers in the village.

Nick leads Harmony to where Dad stands with an arm around me, and soon we're at the center of a murmuring crowd. Dad takes Harmony's hand and pulls her gently toward him until he can put his other arm around her. He senses . . . something, or maybe it's just the protective father in him. In any case, Harmony smiles. She feels safe too, at least for this brief moment.

"They're back!" Chimney shouts from a porch and dashes toward us, and Nick grabs him and swings him around before releasing him to hug me. He's grown taller since we left. That's what my old neighbors always said about me when they hadn't seen me for a while.

I feel old.

The crowd parts to let Orville and Riku through. It's well past Last Meal, and I remember how the villagers used to circle the little pond and chant Odin's name for rain. They don't do it anymore. I was supposed to keep them believing in him. I was supposed to be his buddy.

"Has it rained since we've been gone?" I ask Orville.

"It's a pleasure to see you too!" he says, and we both laugh at our awkward reunion. He opens his arms and wings—the crowd gasps lightly at a sight they've seen numerous times, because how could they not?—and while I hug him, he says, "Yes. It rained shortly after you left. A strange first question, I must say."

So! It will rain without the sky god's involvement. This reinforces my growing sense that we can survive without Odin's interference. I'm about to explain myself when Chimney interrupts.

"Hey, Celeste, why is that girl wearing your scarf over her eyes?" He scrunches his shoulders and I can tell he's trying not to stare at Harmony, but I can also tell everyone else is thinking the same thing.

I introduce Harmony with a vague reference to an injury requiring time to heal—*so much time, and how will I even heal her?* After briefly highlighting what everyone should know about our interactions with the gods and what we can learn through Harmony's chip, I feel a growing sense of anticipation in the crowd.

"They're still working on their army, you say?" Orville asks.

I nod.

"Then, we should attack them before they're ready."

~ **27** ~

THE CROWD AGREES. I look around and see a village united, old and young, male and female, powers and no powers, humans and creatures. This is Vittoria.

Orville addresses the gathering. "Sleep now, friends, for tomorrow we leave our home in order to save it."

They all disperse, and Nick and I lead Harmony into the house where we sit around the kitchen table. The youngest linger. They want to know more about Harmony. They want to see her eyes.

"Let's go, munchkins." Maddie whisks them upstairs and Orville shares the plans they've made in our absence.

"Ah . . . how long have we been gone?" I ask.

"Several long, anxious days," my father says, and then his eyebrows draw together and he closes his lips tightly—his serious face.

"Merts and their team have prepared quite an arsenal of arrows for every bow," Orville says. "We've sharpened shovels and other scrap metal into fearsome weapons. Your father knows a lot about combat from past studies and has shared tactical ideas for both offense and defense. Our drills have been hasty, but we will have an advantage if we take them by surprise. The young ones, with Chimney and

Maddie, have been gathering food for days and are ready to support our march. The weather has been comfortably warm through the nights."

"Wait a minute," I stop him, "we're taking the kids?" The idea startles me.

"It wasn't our initial plan," Mac says, "but as they pointed out to us, most of them have helpful powers. Not a single one wants to stay behind."

"Not even Eenie and her kittens?"

"Not even Eenie and her kittens. She won't hear of Thunder going off without her, and the cubs are nearly Thunder's size already."

"It's true," Teresa says. "You know of Jack's uncanny strength, and what Katie did to that wave before it hit Bridger's wall, well . . . the truth is, we're all in this together, and we've chosen to stay together, for better or worse, and we've been through plenty of worse."

Nick takes my hand under the table, and I see Harmony smile.

"Harmony," Orville speaks softly and places a hand lightly on her arm, "have you heard anything helpful? We have planned for several days travel, but we're hopeful the voices you hear will prepare us for what we'll face when we arrive."

Harmony turns toward Orville's voice. "The sword arms are working in nearly every beast and they're moving as Lilith wants them to move. Something about conducting drills. And Blanche says the army should be returning to the lab soon."

"Sword arms?" Orville asks. Riku strokes his arm distractedly.

I explain how Harmony was afflicted with the mechanization, but only Nick and Harmony and Kumugwe know how I was able to deactivate her.

"And the flying creatures sound vicious," she says. "They have several, maybe five or six. And other voices. Mean voices. Lots of different people besides my sister, who sounds like a very young girl—how can that be?—and Blanche, who sounds . . . uneasy. They're not ready, but I saw what the scientists were able to do during my short time in their submarine." She frowns, and I know she's remembering how they abused Zoya. In a whisper, she says, "They should have to pay for what they've done."

"They will, Harmony," I say. "We'll stop them, and we'll stop whatever army they're gathering." I think about Bridger and how everything around him must horrify him.

My father nods his agreement. "She's right. An army controlled by fear and mechanical devices can be defeated."

"If we're planning to move out tomorrow, then let me find the exact location of the lab," I say. "The ravens gave me an image of where they are, and I recognized some of the surroundings. They're somewhere east of the cave, Orville. You remember the cave, right?"

He smiles a sad smile. He remembers.

"No! It's too dangerous," Nick says. "It's dark and those flying things and—"

"I can see in the dark. I can fly fast and high, and they'll never be expecting me. I need to do this, Nick. We need to know how far down the coast they are. I'll be back before you're asleep, I promise."

I take his hand and he frowns at me for an instant, but then his eyes soften.

"It would help to know where they are," he says.

"And hey," I try to sound upbeat, "I have this nifty spear. What could go wrong?"

Harmony snaps her face toward me and without a word, tells me never to ask that question. Her demeanor is unsettling.

"Oh, and before I leave, have you talked about traveling in different ways?" I ask.

"Different?" Riku asks.

"Yes, like, not just on land. Do we still have all those boats Bridger made before I threw this spear into the water?" It's strange that the spear is mine. I look across the table and notice my father nodding at me with a satisfied grin on his face.

"Yes, they're behind the last house at the end of the road," Mac says.

"Well, based on where I think the lab is, it's not far from the water. Orville and I are the only ones who can fly, so we're limited by how many we can take by air. The animals and some of the humans can travel by ground, and some of the older villagers could escort the younger ones by water. We should use everything that could be an asset along the way."

"By land, sea, and air. That's my girl! Yes, Celeste, we've talked about this in our planning."

"Oh! Of course you have!" I feel a little foolish, like I've just told an English teacher how to punctuate a sentence. "And I'll know more after I find the lab."

"My, my. You do remember some of what I taught you during our camping trips." Dad's eyes look wistful.

"More than you know, Dad."

What would I have done without his compass lessons, his astronomy lessons, his campfire cooking lessons? I cringe when I recall skewering the rodents near the cave after Orville rescued me from the sandcastle. I see Harmony's eyebrows rise high above the scarf, and can only imagine she's recalling the same experience through me. Now that she knows me, she must feel guilty for nearly killing me in there. She didn't know any better, though. She's just a child raised by creatures of the water.

"Okay. Off I go, then." I stand up and Nick stands with me. We're still holding hands. Dad raises one eyebrow.

"Be watchful, daughter. And return as you promised."

They all stand as Nick and I leave the room, except for Harmony, who's no longer smiling. Nick walks with me outside and stops me in the middle of the road.

"How about Omega?" he says.

"Omega what?"

"For your spear's name. I remember something about Alpha and Omega, the beginning and the end. Something to do with foreign letters. Omega's the last letter. Let this spear help you bring an end to our troubles."

"Omega. It's perfect. Thanks, Nick." I'm afraid to look into his eyes, but I do. And when he looks into my eyes, I know what will happen next.

The tingling starts before his lips touch mine, and when I feel the heat in his eager kiss, I start to melt.

~ 28 ~

WHEN HE PEELS AWAY from me, it hurts.

"Celeste? Celeste? Open your eyes, Celeste. Come on! Please, breathe!"

Why is he shaking me? Why can't I see him? Oh, yeah. I should open my eyes . . . and I should breathe.

"Holy moly!" I say. "What happened?" I'm on the ground, collapsed in Nick's arms. He holds me like I held him when Ryder and I healed his brain. "Did I hurt you?" I can't bear to see him hurt again.

"No, no . . . well . . . not really."

"What do you mean, not really?" I break from his arms and stand up, but I feel dizzy and disoriented for several moments. He jumps up to steady me.

"I'm fine. I'm fine, really," he says, shaking his head. "It's just that when we, you know, kissed, I kinda felt like I lost you for a while. It made my heart squeeze a little, and then I felt you falling. It was almost like you were falling out of me, and taking tiny pieces of me with you. It felt like an ache, but I'm fine. Are you okay?" He brushes the hair from my face and then pulls me back into his arms.

It's awkward hugging him with a spear in one hand, but I guess that means I didn't drop it when I fell. Maybe it didn't let me drop it.

"Yeah, yes, I think so."

"You shouldn't go. We're not in any immediate danger—you said so yourself—and I can't even remember how long it's been since we've slept. Stay. Please."

But I couldn't sleep even if Harmony sang me her most soothing lullaby. "I can't. Every moment we wait gives our enemies more time to grow their army."

Enemies. What a strong word for people I've never even met. How could there be enemies anymore among those who survived The Event?

But Harmony's parents didn't just survive The Event, they caused it. At least that's what I've been led to believe. And if it's true, then I have to find out why. And I have to know we can stop them from creating more havoc on the planet.

"I'll be back before you're asleep. Watch out for Harmony, will you?"

"You know, if I thought it would keep you here, I'd stop time right now. How is it that you're immune from my power?" It's a question with no answer expected. He smiles and doesn't let go.

"Maybe I wish I wasn't," I say, and I feel the heat rise to my cheeks. He'd be able to stop me, then, and maybe I wouldn't feel so compelled to keep leaving him, to keep searching for answers.

It would be an easy choice to wait until the army comes to us and have Nick stop time before they attack, but I'm not convinced the fluxes have completely ceased. I get the impression no one is convinced, which means we can't count on consistent powers.

And what if the enemy is immune too?

I disengage reluctantly and take a small step away from Nick's warmth. "All right, then, Omega," I say in a theatrical voice, holding the spear up to the sky, "take me to their leaders!"

"Very funny," Nick says, and he takes a small step back as well. "Stay *away* from their leaders. You're just going to find the lab, remember?"

"I remember. See you soon," I say, and lift into the sky.

It's peaceful up here in the atmosphere. I'd forgotten how everything appears more beautiful. It's dark below me, but the stars above cast intricate shadows on the planet and reflect glowing ripples on the water. I could lose myself up here.

I did, for a while, with Odin.

The thought of him makes me wary, and I search the sky for his ravens. They took me to him a lifetime ago, and I could have stayed there in Asgard—or Oblivia, as we once called the majestic place far removed from this planet. I could have eaten my fill without labor and played with the wolves, slept in buoyant clouds and delivered rain where I chose to. I could have lived forever in the brilliantly striated clouds in the heavens and done whatever I pleased.

Why did I want to escape? And why am I holding this spear? Where am I? In my confusion, I start to fall.

"Celeste!" I hear Harmony's voice in my head. "The laboratory. Find the laboratory and return to us. Nick is drowsy."

Of course! I escaped for Nick and for the others. Being in the atmosphere like this plays with my head, but I'm no god, and I have no desire to live a god's life.

What's a life with little fear of death? Knowing we'll die someday makes every moment more meaningful. And what's the value of anything if everything can be possessed? What's real in a realm where everything is just a game?

I get control of myself and descend until I'm closer to the planet's surface, where I recall the last vision the ravens shared with me. The submarine was grounded on a beach a distance east of the village—beyond the cave where I recovered from starvation and lost friends—and I could see a structure not far from the water's edge. That's where I'm going.

I study my spear as I fly. It needs a purpose. I probably shouldn't put off this decision, but what should I ask of it? Does it work like a magical lantern holding a genie? Will I get three wishes? And if so, what wish would be the most helpful to me, and to my community, if I'm allowed only one?

"Omega?" I address the spear as if it's listening. "I've chosen a purpose for you." It might be my imagination, but I feel it vibrate in my hand. Harmony was right. It's waiting. "You must never allow me to use you for a selfish purpose. Do you accept?"

The waves of orichalcum in Omega's shaft glow brilliantly and I feel happy inside. It answered my question. It feels alive in my hand, and I'm struck by the sensation this spear has always been mine.

I pass over the collapsed cave, the burial ground for Floyd—the loveable boxer who ran with Ranger's pack on the other side of the big water until I brought him to this side—and two of Eenie's kittens. A wave of sorrow replaces the happy feeling I was enjoying.

"Please tell me they didn't suffer," I say to Omega, and it glows again, though not as brightly, and the burden of my sorrow lifts from me. "Thank you," I whisper.

Not too much farther down the coast, about a day's walk, an unnatural shape captures my attention. It must be the laboratory. It looks a little blurry, almost like there's a heat mirage around it.

I hover, and I grip Omega more firmly. I scan the space above the structure for fliers, but see none, so I advance slowly. I could go back to the village—I've found what I came looking for—but the more information I can take back, the more prepared we'll be to face whatever's in there.

I'll just fly above it and dissolve myself to infiltrate the building, the same way I got through the cracks in Kumugwe's castle when I first dispersed. After all the times I've done it, this transformation feels natural to me.

But what about Omega?

"Omega, can you transform your particles to go through tiny cracks in solid objects? This is something I can do, and I need to do it once we're over the building."

Omega shakes in my hand and turns icy cold. I guess that means *no*. As much as I hate to do it, I retreat a distance from the building and bury Omega under sand and some loose brush.

"Stay here. I'll be right back." I half expect Omega to rise up and fly to my hand, and I'm a little disappointed when it doesn't.

When I'm over the building and look down at it, I notice the same blurry illusion I saw from the ground. I'll get a little closer before I dissolve. Nick was right about my needing sleep.

"Y'OUCH!" I slap my hands over my mouth, but what the heck just happened? It's like I've flown into a wall, but I can't see one. I'm standing on a surface I can't see either. This is not good. I should leave, but I'm so close.

I walk cautiously, sliding my hand along an invisible wall on my left, when the surface below my feet ends without warning and I fall to a level closer to the rooftop. This is disconcerting.

I feel for the wall to my left on this level, and then walk more cautiously, sliding one foot at a time to my right, my right hand searching for an unseen barrier on the other side of this blurry passageway. It takes a while, but I find it. I shuffle along this wall until I feel it turn a corner, and then another. And then I realize my mistake.

I'm trapped in an invisible three-dimensional maze.

~ **29** ~

I HAVE TO GET out of here. I leap into the air, forgetting about the invisible barrier above me, and smack my head hard. Sitting in a heap on another surface, I chastise myself for being so reckless.

Backtrack. That's what I'll do. I try to remember the turns I've taken, but I'm already turned around, and I can't feel or see the wall I followed on this level. Am I even on the same level, or could I have fallen through another hole after my hasty escape attempt? It seems like I'm closer to the rooftop.

Panic rises from my gut. It tastes like burning saltwater.

Where are you, Celeste? Harmony's voice startles me. *He's asleep, and you're not here. They're all asleep. All but me. They tried to stay awake, but these topside bodies are so very weak. You promised you'd return before they fell asleep. Aren't promises things you're supposed to keep?*

Her words make me feel uneasy—everything about my current situation makes me feel uneasy—but if I can hear her, she can probably hear me too. I close my eyes and answer her.

Yes, Harmony. Promises are things you're supposed to keep. And I'd be home right now, but I'm trapped over the laboratory. I must sound crazy. *Please be patient. I'll find a way out.*

She doesn't answer, but I hear her whimpering.

I will, I—don't say promise—*I'll find a way and I'll be there before they wake up.* I wish I sounded more convincing, but all I can see when I look above me is a dark blur, and I can't keep hitting my head. The fastest way out might be down, through holes in the surfaces beneath my feet. And if I'm honest with myself, I've already made the decision to get inside the lab.

Invisible barriers thwart me constantly, and every time I fall through a hole I'm unprepared. Fortunately, my blundering doesn't seem to make any noise in here. My eyes are wide open, but I might as well be blind in this disturbing maze.

What if I dissolved? Could I seep through these passageways faster, or would my particles become hopelessly scattered, disjointed to the point of not being able to regroup back into me because—where would *I* be? I don't even know where I am.

I can't take that chance.

Shuffle, bump, turn, fall—if I knew how far I'd fall each time, I could prepare myself to land more gracefully, but every level seems to vary in height. And when I get to the rooftop . . . then what? The building appeared blurry from the ground too, so this maze extends all around it.

And I don't have Omega with me. I could have asked it questions about what's inside, but I have to see things with my own eyes. I have to discover answers by myself. The hard way.

It's why I left the children's home the way I did.

Patience. It's what I told Harmony to have. *Breathe, Celeste, and keep moving.*

Some of these passages take me far from the rooftop before turning back, and I keep hoping I'll eventually fall to the ground, but it doesn't happen. I'm reminded of the slippery seaweed hallways in Harmony's sandcastle. If Orville hadn't rescued me, I would have died in there.

But wait! Odin was the one who delivered Orville to me in the form of a wind-up flying frog. He knew I was in trouble. Does he know I'm in trouble now?

I escaped from Asgard without saying goodbye. I left him misshapen in the underwater castle. I could've helped him, but I didn't. Why would he ever feel inclined to help me again? *Keep moving, Celeste.*

Just when I think I'm almost there, a passageway takes me far, far away from the building. There have been no turns, no bumps, no holes for a long way, and I'm tense with anticipation for my next drop. When I finally do hit a wall and turn back, I notice the sky is less dark. It's almost dawn. I'll never make it out before the village awakens.

What will they think? What will they do? What will I do if the beings in this building see me trapped in their ingenious maze? I'll dissolve in place, that's what I'll do.

But for now, *just . . . keep . . . moving.*

I'm finally over the roof again. I see Bridger's forced handiwork in building this structure. There are many gaps for me to infiltrate once I get there. If I can find out what's happening inside without them seeing me, I can relay the information to Harmony and—

I drop through the last hole onto the rooftop, sirens blare, searing pain stings my feet, and everything goes black.

~ 30 ~

"**WELL, WELL, THURSTON,** who do we have here?"

"Oh, Lilith, I don't know. Maybe another lost one come to help us?"

"New girl! Wanna see the new girl, Mommy!"

"Blanche, would you *please* keep this incessant child away from me!"

"Yes, ma'am. Come here, Sharon. Let's leave the new girl alone."

"But I wanna see her! She looks like—"

"Put that child in the room with the boy. Do it now."

"Yes, ma'am."

~ ~ ~ ~ ~

I hear their voices as if in a dream, or a nightmare, and the implications of what I've done hit me hard. If I'm identified as being from the village, I've just put my friends in danger. They'll be coming this way soon, today, and without any help from me. My father will be worried sick over my absence. And Nick . . . I never should have promised a quick return. Maybe I never should have left them.

But if I'd stayed, we'd all be walking into combat blind. Here, I can learn how to defeat these scheming people.

Blanche is here. I have to be cautious. I'm not sure what game she might be playing. I know she recognizes me, but she didn't say anything. I take it as a sign she won't tell them about me, at least not yet, so I won't act like I know her either. She'd be in danger then too.

There's an odd, sterile smell in this place, like the air particles have been charged with alcohol but they still retain traces of disease.

Something's covering my eyes. My head aches and my feet feel hot. I try to sit up, but my hands and feet are bound to whatever platform they've put me on.

"Don't move yet, girlie." It's Lilith—I remember her voice from the visions Harmony shared with me, and how could I ever forget it? It's the same voice Sharon spoke with when she was controlling the village as the Overleader. I shiver when I recall the spear Sharon had me hold and how it made me relive the nightmare of the day I lost my family. It was the Spear of Sorrow, then. And now it's buried outside in the sand, useless to me.

If supernatural spears have feelings, then it's waiting for my return. And so are my friends.

Is the child Blanche was told to take away the same Sharon who instilled such fear in so many people back in the village? She sounds like a three-year-old, but I remember Harmony saying her sister sounded like a little girl from the voices she heard through the chip in her brain. Is it possible to grow younger on this unstable planet?

It's hard not to cringe when Lilith speaks. "You've had quite a fall, and we're going to keep you here until we know a little more about you." This sounds more like a threat than concern for my wellbeing, and her breath—too close to my nose—smells like dead fish. "We'll leave your eyes covered until you've had time to recover."

I suspect they covered my eyes so I can't see their laboratory—but what if my eyes are actually injured? I move them back and forth beneath my eyelids and they feel okay. Poor Harmony. I'll never shake my guilt over blinding her. Seems like I deserve this.

"So, tell me, girlie, how is it that you landed on my rooftop? Did a big old birdie pluck you away and drop you from the sky?" I can hear the sneer in her stinking voice.

I shake my head slowly and say nothing.

"What's the matter? Cat got your tongue? Could it be you came from the little village near my old home?"

It's a question she could ask Blanche. I hope she won't. Would Blanche lie for me if Lilith does ask? I don't know. I don't know who Blanche has become yet.

"It'll be nice to get back to our little house for a bit, won't it, Thurston?"

"Uh-huh," he says.

She has no idea their little house was sucked into an enormous hole in the earth after I took the spear from it. After Blanche helped me take it. And I honestly thought returning it to the sea was the key to saving our planet.

The ooze cleared, at least for a while, but it was just an effect caused by the fluxes, probably while Zoya was growing weaker and more unstable. That poor creature!

How could Blanche have left the village for these appalling people?

"Speak up, girlie. Do you have any more friends who might be dropping in on us today? Or did you run away from your friends and home? And where, do tell, is your home?" Her voice makes me feel prickly all over and I really want to dissolve, but I can't. Not yet.

"Dropping in on us today," Thurston repeats, and chuckles. "That's funny, cuz she fell on the roof." He has a man's voice, but sounds childlike.

"I . . . can't remember," I whisper. Since I don't yet know the extent of my injuries, faking amnesia is my safest response. How could I be a threat if I don't remember anything?

"You can't remember how you landed on my rooftop, or where your home is?" Lilith's words are sharp and clipped.

"Oh, Lilith, let the girl rest. That was quite a zap she got." He chuckles again and repeats the word *zap* a few times. A hand pats the top of my head—Thurston's hand, I presume—and I question his mental competence.

Maybe it's just Lilith I need to worry about.

I hear footsteps approaching.

"Sharon's with Bridger. He'll watch her." It's Blanche. "Your army is back and they're ready for your instruction. I'll watch this girl."

"Good," Lilith says. "The final drill. Find out what you can from her."

"Yes, ma'am."

"She must remember where her home is. We'll start by subduing your old village, Blanche, and then we'll defeat hers."

Blanche doesn't correct her. I breathe more easily, though the smell in here is vile.

"One by one, they'll fall to me." Lilith cackles.

"One by one and two by two, roses are red and so are you," Thurston mumbles, and then chuckles inanely.

My heart pounds in my ears as the clip-clop and shuffle of Lilith's and Thurston's feet echo down what sounds like a hallway. I can't move, I can't see. I could free myself by dissolving, but I have to find out what Blanche knows, and how this lab functions.

It's quiet for a very long time. Which one of us will break the silence? I hear a chair being pulled up by my side and I brace. I feel vulnerable not being able to see or move. It's dreadful.

"What are you going to do, Blanche? You already know everything there is to tell her about me. But you didn't. I feel like I should thank you."

"Shut up, will you? I don't know what I'm going to do. How'd you know we were here? And how'd you get through the maze?" There's a hint of excitement in her voice, but without seeing her, I don't know how to interpret it.

"Never mind that. How much time do we have before they return?"

"I don't know. Lilith could be out there all day, or she could come back looking for answers soon. Why are you here, Celeste?"

"I'll ask you the same question." Before she answers, I have to get this thing off my eyes. I have to see her face. I focus on the pungent smell, which makes me queasy, and use it to my advantage. I grimace and make myself gag. "I'm going to throw up! Untie me, quick."

I hear the chair scratch the floor as she pushes it back, and the binding on my right hand is loosened until I can pull it free. I taste the bile rise in my throat as I turn onto my left side just in time for my insides to heave and splash onto the floor.

"Gross, Celeste!"

"I'm pretty sure you've seen worse things, Blanche." I pull the blindfold off my head but I'm afraid to open my eyes, afraid of what I might see, or not see. I pull at the restraint on my left hand until it's freed and she doesn't stop me.

Slowly, so slowly, I open my eyelids just enough to let in a little light. Blurred shapes and dull colors come into focus as I open them a little more until I'm confident I haven't lost my vision. When I let them open fully, the first thing I see is a worried expression on Blanche's face.

She's changed. She looks . . . lost.

I'm hopeful she'll be able to find herself again, the self she was before children were left to make all the decisions.

~ 31 ~

BLANCHE LOOKS HORRIBLY THIN. I want to be angry at her, but seeing what I've seen so far, I can only imagine how grim her life has been since she left the village.

"The last time I saw you," I say, freeing my feet from the bindings—she still doesn't stop me,—"you helped me take the spear from the Overleader's house."

Does she remember that day? She does. She looks at me like a child who knows she's done something wrong.

"Blanche? You can come back home, you know. I'll help you."

She looks confused and angry. "I thought you were dead. You never came back." She turns away from my gaze.

Did she want me to return? Would she have stayed in the village if I had? My attention is drawn to some kind of control panel with glowing buttons and wires mounted on a wall not far behind her. I have to get to it.

"I tried to get back," I say, meandering toward the panel. Trying to get back—my motivating inspiration for more times than I want to remember.

Blanche follows me, and I change the subject. "Where's Bridger? Is he all right?" I remember his little voice calling for help from the apple tree at the children's home a lifetime ago. It kills me not to grab him right now and flee, but there are things in this place I'm certain will help me defeat these insane scientists. I'll bring him home, but not before I do some damage here.

"Bridger's fine." She looks guilty. Her forehead wrinkles and I can tell she's hesitant to ask her next question. "Have you seen . . ."

She can't even say her brother's name.

"Yes. Chimney's doing well. He's really a remarkable kid. He and Nick risked their lives to find me. But he misses you, you know. He's grown." We're standing right in front of the glowing panel.

Blanche inhales sharply and I see relief flash across her face. She's guarding her emotions. I want to ask her why, why would she leave him for these horrible people? But there's no time for that. There's no time for any more chatter.

Her body shakes and I see she's struggling not to cry. "I'm so, so tired, Celeste."

I put my hands on her shoulders and I want to tell her the villagers are on their way when a door opens at the end of the hallway and I hear the clip-clop of Lilith's shoes. Simultaneously, Harmony's voice in my head startles me— her timing is horrible. The villagers are well on their way, and she wants to know what I've found.

No time to answer her.

I act fast, dissolving and spreading myself throughout the room, infiltrating the control panel and the wires and the walls. It's so easy for me, this act of dissolving, and each time I do it, it feels more instinctive. More . . . me.

Blanche is startled by my sudden disappearance.

"Lilith! Come here! Fast!" she yells, and for a moment, I fear what she might say.

Lilith speeds her way into the room and her eyes look cruel.

Blanche intercepts her at the empty platform and, dramatically holding her hands out to her sides as if to protect herself, stares at my sick mess on the floor. Her actions are bizarre, and while I try to interpret what my particles are feeling in these wires, I'm also watching her. Not watching, exactly. When I'm in this state it's more like knowing. It's as if all of my senses become one and I see, feel, hear, smell, taste . . . know everything.

"You better have a good explanation for—"

"She was here! She was just here! She . . . I mean, *it* . . . just flashed like a lightning bolt and dissolved into this disgusting goo! What *is* this?" She steps back from the mess as if it's threatening her.

So, she does want to come back home. And there's still a spark of life lurking in her weary body. I'm impressed by her improvisation.

Where are you? Harmony's voice interrupts me again—it feels like an invasion of my privacy this time, and I have to stay focused on these wires. *Are you in the lab?*

She's blind, but she's seeing what I'm seeing. If this were a dream, it would make more sense, but it's not. How I wish it were a dream, along with everything that's happened since before The Event. Just a nightmare I could wake from.

I feel intensely thirsty, but it's not my body that thirsts. It's hers.

Overwhelmed by the disparate tasks demanding my attention at the moment, I feel myself trying to snap back into my body, but that would be disastrous. I have to be in many places, and it's confusing. I force different particles of my being to focus on each task. It's difficult, and the more I try to separate my particles, the stronger they want to stay connected.

"Whatever it is, destroy it!" Pointing a crooked finger at the mess, Lilith shouts at Blanche before heading to the control panel, where a part of me waits. I'm stunned Lilith didn't question Blanche about her story, but then again, her work has been creating anomalies ever since The Event, and possibly before.

Get into the water, fast, another part of me tells Harmony. She's out of her element, and if she weakens, I'm afraid I might too. *And yes, I'm in the lab.* That's all I can tell her. Things are happening too fast.

Patterns in the wires start to make sense to me, and when Lilith reaches for the panel, I'm ready.

"This'll show any other interlopers," she cackles, but when her hand makes contact with a button, some of my particles drag an electrical current to her sweaty finger. "Mother of Mephistopheles!" she shouts, and I smell singed hair.

I thought the current would kill her.

Blanche rushes over, but keeps her distance from the frazzled woman. "What can I do?" she asks.

"What can you do? What can you do? I told you to destroy the interloper! Can you do that, girl?" Lilith screams at Blanche, and I sense the scientist's embarrassment at her predicament. She plans to increase the size and complexity of the maze field, but now she's afraid to touch the controls.

She should be afraid.

My particles feel cool and refreshed—Harmony must be in the water. I sizzle sections of the circuitry controlling the ingenious maze and smoke wafts from the panel.

"My maze!" Lilith screams, and runs past Blanche and down the hall.

She doesn't know it yet, but her maze is gone.

Blanche looks around the room—she's searching for me—should I show myself again? It feels too dangerous, but it also feels like Blanche is about to break down. She has to keep Bridger and Sharon safe.

"Celeste? Are you in here? If you are, I just want to say, be careful." Her voice is strained.

I snap back into my body and approach her purposefully. I need answers. Blanche jumps when she sees me, her eyes wide.

"What's Lilith's objective, Blanche? What does she want? And fast." I hear shouting outside the building.

"Probably the same thing I used to want. I wanted everyone to listen to me, to do what I told them to do. I wanted to be everyone's stern, protective mother, like the one I lost in The Event. Lilith sees herself as the perfect mother for this new planet, but if anyone fights back, her army is programmed to kill. Those who pledge their allegiance to her will live, but she'll dictate their lives."

The perfect mother. And she abandoned her own children.

"Why would anyone agree to that?"

"Because she'll control the food supply. You'd be surprised what people and animals will do when they're starving."

"So why haven't you stopped her?" It's probably an unfair question to ask someone who's managed to keep her head straight in an environment saturated with threat.

"I can't get near her. She's paranoid about being touched by anyone other than Thurston, and she's surrounded herself with a force field like the one she created for the maze. Thurston's the only one who can get near her."

Why would she allow such a feeble-minded man near her? I suppose even a madwoman needs a human touch now and then. And he's certainly no threat to her.

"I'm going to find a way to stop them, Blanche. Can I count on you to keep Bridger and Sharon safe?" I can't believe I feel responsible for Sharon, but she's just a child. Maybe there's hope for her.

"Yes, I'll do what I can, and Celeste? I'm sorry—"

I dissolve before she finishes her sentence.

Before I float from the building, I find the room where Bridger is playing with a toddler. He's creating building blocks and intricate structures to entertain Sharon, who's regressed in age since mere moments ago.

What happens when there's no age left to return to? I can't worry about that. This could be the planet's way of rebalancing without the gods, though I don't know where Odin is right now.

Bridger looks happy, playing with her. I want to enter his mind and tell him he's not alone, help is coming, he'll be home soon, but I feel like it might frighten him. In an odd way, I also feel like it might be an unwarranted invasion, like the way I've been feeling lately when Harmony jumps into my consciousness. And what could he do with the information anyway?

Instead, I wrap myself around Bridger and Sharon in a touchless, invisible embrace, my particles brushing lightly against those surrounding them, and I hear them laugh.

It's time to stop the madwoman and her army of monstrosities.

~ **32** ~

ONCE OUTSIDE, I spread myself thin over the ruckus below to assess the situation. Lilith is dragging Thurston by the hand back into the building, presumably to have him figure out what caused the maze to fail. She won't touch the control panel again, and Thurston will never discover my vandalism.

I fried it beyond repair.

Three of the bat creatures are flying circles around the perimeter above me and give no indication they sense my presence. I see two of them hanging upside down from limbs of a tree near the building. They're most likely the night guards, though I didn't see them when I arrived. Maybe they're not so dedicated to their tasks when Lilith isn't watching.

For the first time, I see for myself the horde of mechanical blobs, more than a hundred, I'd guess. They're moving and shooting swords from their limbs, controlled by a disheveled man standing a distance away, and it's truly a horrifying sight. The humans—I count thirty-nine dirty, sinewy bodies—grapple with one another and make thrusting motions with various sharp weapons.

Do any of these survivors know how many children are in the village they plan to vanquish?

I see what you're seeing, Harmony's voice startles me again and I'm glad I decided against communicating with Bridger. This does feel like an invasion. *I sense where you are and will guide the villagers. We should be there before dusk tomorrow. I'll tell them you're more help to us there.*

A blind girl is leading my village. My village. Our village. My new home. I won't let these creatures and their leader subjugate us. *Please tell our friends I'm all right and will do everything in my power to incapacitate this army before you get here.*

I want to fly to them and ease their journey, but Harmony's right. I can do far more to help them here. At a minimum, I can stall Lilith's planned departure. I can disable her blobs. If not all, then many.

You have a plan. I can feel it. But why can't you just defeat Lilith? Why can't you stop her? The army's nothing without her, and the man who was my birth father isn't that man anymore. He's nothing without her either.

I tell her about Lilith's personal force field and the maze. I don't have any brilliant ideas yet how I'll breach Lilith's protective shield, but if I can disable her creatures and we can neutralize the rest of her army when the villagers arrive, she'll have to concede defeat. She'll just have to.

And I do have a plan. When I removed the weaponized pieces from you, Harmony, I left the chip that controls the basic movement of your arms and legs, the one that also allows you to hear what's being said. Now I know what I'm looking for in the machines. Tonight, when training is over and Lilith is sleeping, I'll do my work. When I'm done, her army won't move an inch. Can our people defeat the humans and the bat creatures? Based on what I know, they're the only ones capable of acting independently.

Yes. We have archers and children with powers, but—

But what?

But they say their powers are inconsistent.

I feared as much, but didn't want to express it. Why are their powers fluctuating when mine seem to grow stronger every day?

The only power I see in the humans here is their cruel, hungry aggression, I say, hoping to bolster her courage. Some amount of superhuman power beats none.

One more thing, she says. *There were sightings of a monstrous dragonfly after you left last night and today, again, while we travel. Your father says her name is Noor, and she helped you in the past, but she hasn't made contact yet.*

Noor! What's her purpose in this ludicrous world? She could wipe out this entire army with one fiery breath!

She's probably looking for me, I say. *I'll find her! She could be our answer!*

We'll continue our advance, Harmony says. *Orville flies high around us to spot danger, the children are in boats hitched behind strong rowers, and the animals and other beings follow the shoreline near me. They have me on a metal horse they call Layla. I just wish her friend Lou would keep quiet.*

If only I could see through her eyes, but when I try, all I see is green—my scarf around her hollowed eyes. Does she feel safe on this journey with strangers, a journey with a goal of neutralizing—no, of killing her birth parents? When I consider she's never had a real family besides the sea creatures and an unlikely, irascible father figure, it makes me sad. But then again, most of us have had to create new families since The Event.

And who decides what a *real* family is anymore?

It feels like Harmony has broken her connection with me. There's a lightness in my particles that's not there when she talks in my mind.

Where's my mind when I'm spread thin like this? The idea amuses me, but I have to keep my focus. I can't lose myself like I nearly did last night. I actually wanted to lose myself in the heavens. The feeling still tugs at me.

Noor. I need to find the dragonfly who saved me from Odin's ravens just to drop me into Kumugwe's realm. What does she expect me to learn from the horrors of the situation unfolding below? Does she expect anything from me? She wanted me to learn what was happening in the sea and help Harmony stop Zoya's torment, which I did. And now what? She may have been unable to navigate the water below its surface, but she's certainly able to command the world topside.

Will she come to my aid this time?

I float high, high above the turmoil below until the building is the size of a mustard seed.

Noor! I summon her with my dispersed being.

Nothing.

I snap back into my body—my mouth voice might be able to get her attention this time—and I'm surprised again to see I'm still wearing a dress. Where does it go when I dissolve? Does it disperse too? Maybe Noor can tell me.

"Noor!" I shout her name with all my being, and the sound echoes through the heavens like thunder.

But just as she didn't come to me when Nick was dying, she doesn't come to me now.

~ **33** ~

I COULD JUST STAY way up here. Like Blanche, I'm tired too. But I've made a commitment to my friends, to my dad, to Nick, and it would be wrong to leave them all . . . again. I fear my comings and goings have distressed Nick the most. Will there ever come a time I might hope to live a peaceful life with him by my side?

I disperse and descend before the magic of this serene atmosphere keeps hold of my particles. I should just go after Lilith—she's back outside, gathering her makeshift army in neat rows facing her. Thurston may be the only person who can touch her, but my particles have infiltrated human and god and all states of matter. I should have done this the moment I awoke from the shock.

This is it. I'll enter her core and do what I did to the control panel in the lab—I'll damage her biological wiring. Her heart will stop beating and that will be the end of her terror. First, though, I wait to hear what she'll say. If any of her humans are truly aligned with her goals, I'll need to know her plans.

"At first light tomorrow, we march!" Lilith stands like a stiff toy soldier and screeches her announcement to the dead and undead.

Do the mechanized blobs understand her words? Do they care? How could they?

I expect to hear a rousing cheer, but the blobs have no mouths and the hungry humans just want the job done so they can eat. There's no true loyalty here.

"Tonight, my kiddiwinks will gather on the far side of the building to be guarded by you batkins," she points to the circling creatures, "and the rest of you shall eat and sleep inside. You must be strong for the days of marching ahead and our ultimate victory over our first village."

The humans look surprised. They've evidently never stepped foot inside the building. I wait for her to say something about the protective maze, but she doesn't.

"Do as I say! To your places!" She claps her hands and then manipulates a device and the blobs start moving to the other side of the building. The humans approach the building skittishly, their hands in front of them. They've obviously experienced the invisible maze.

"Go in straightaway. I'll re-arm the shield when we're inside."

So, she won't tell them the truth about the force field, and by keeping them inside, they'll never discover the truth— that she's been compromised. This is good. Lilith looks nervous, and the humans won't get in my way.

I float a distance above her. She chuckles mirthlessly and Thurston giggles beside her. They watch to ensure everyone obeys, and as the last human enters the building, I make my move, sending my particles toward her wicked eyes.

What's this? An arm's length away from her, my closest particles begin to vibrate uncontrollably, and my physical hand starts to appear. NO! This can't be! A ball of static electricity hangs sparking in the space between her eyes and my hand, and I retreat quickly.

It's true. Even I can't get near her.

"Ball of fire!" Thurston points to where I've been and giggles.

"To the lab, fool!" Lilith grabs his hand and pulls him into the building.

What do I do? My hand particles tingle unpleasantly, but at least they didn't see my physical hand appear. Whatever she's doing to the space surrounding herself is more powerful than the maze she created for the building, probably because her space is far more compact. But that doesn't explain why Thurston is unaffected.

In any case, they're all inside, and the blobs outside are protected only by flying creatures who can't see me. The hundred-strong force looks like one gigantic, failed gelatin mold, the whole mass of them quivering slightly in the cool breeze coming from the darkening water.

I remember the holiday creations Mom would make in fruit-shaped copper molds filled with marshmallows and pieces of chopped fruit and sometimes nuts. I loved poking them when they flopped out of the mold. Watching them jiggle, we'd all laugh.

I miss my mom. The thought of her pulls my particles upward and I have to fight to bring them back to the task at hand, to these disastrous molds that smell of salt and sulfur.

I infiltrate the first blob directly through its translucent body and find the master chip immediately. My particles surround it and rip it right out, leaving a small hole that seals back together with internal gelatinous goo. It makes a soft little *shgluck* sound, and I wait to see if the bats hear it. If they do, they don't let on.

I shove the chip deep into the sand under the blob's legs. There's no need to remove the weaponized pieces. When Lilith commands her army to move, she'll be startled when they don't obey. She'll push buttons and have her other trusted humans push their buttons, and eventually someone will push the weapons button. Her blobs will massacre themselves.

I'm glad Lilith's plan is to leave in the morning, because this process will take some time. If I could detach my particles into different clusters, I could spread out and finish this job in no time. It would be like having octopus arms—each cluster could work independently.

And if Nick were here, he could stop time, and then the two of us could destroy it all. If only he were here with me. But no more ifs.

I focus on sending a detached cluster of myself to the next blob. At first, I feel an unpleasant pull, as if someone were tugging on my arm and it was about to pop from my shoulder socket. Only a glimmering filament of my particles connects the cluster to the rest of me.

Focus! I tell myself, but just as the cluster is about to detach completely, my particles scream in pain and pull it back.

Evidently I can spread myself only so thin.

And so, on to the next blob I go, repeating the chip removal process one by one as the oblivious bats—first three, then two, then only one—soar in sloppy circles above. On through the night, *shgluck, shgluck, shgluck*, I disable one after the other until I sense the darkness ready to retreat.

I should be exhausted, but I'm not. Nick and the others are close—I feel it!—and I'm confident in our numbers and abilities. Adrenaline makes my particles glow, though the sleepy bat above doesn't notice. I feel alive!

Throughout the long night, not a sound has escaped the building. But as I tear the final chip from the last blob, an infant's plaintive cry breaks the silence, just before first light.

~ 34 ~

I DON'T STICK AROUND to see what Lilith will do once she discovers her ridiculous toy army is already defeated. The fact that she thought these creatures would be a powerful force proves how irrational she's become.

The humans and bats may fight for her, but I already have reason to question their resolve. And once her people see our children, well, if there are any remnants of humanity in their blood, I suspect they'll at least pause.

I'm excited to reunite with Nick, my father, my friends, but I'm anxious too. Lives are at stake.

As I approach the place I've buried my spear, I snap into my body. For the first time, I'm aware of the heaviness of my arms, my legs, my physical being, and it feels odd. I look back toward the lab and see one weary bat still circling the immovable blobs.

Lilith should unleash her wrath upon the winged creatures for their negligence. Then we'd have only humans to confront when the time comes.

Omega rises from the sand without my having to dig and glows as if telling me it's happy to be in my hand again. Could it be the key, once again, to stopping the remaining threat to our village, at least for a while? Maybe it can penetrate Lilith's shield. It wouldn't be a selfish act to kill her if that's what it takes to save our village, but I hope it won't come to that.

Maybe she'll surrender.

I've never killed a person before, but she has. Her actions have killed more than we'll ever know, and with no sign of remorse. I have to remember that.

I'm fooling myself to think she'll surrender.

I take to the air, glad my powers haven't yet fluctuated, and in no time at all, I see emerald wings glittering in the first rays of daylight.

"Orville!" I call to him. He hovers for a moment, looks around him and below in every direction for any possible threat, and then joins me in the air.

"Celeste! How much longer until we encounter our foe? We're prepared."

"It shouldn't be long at all. Let's gather on the beach and rest a bit—you look like you've flown through the night."

"No one wanted to stop. It's good to see you again, Celeste."

Orville flies to the boats and gestures them to shore, and I approach Harmony, whose clothes are drenched with sea water. I land and walk beside Layla—the gigantic metal horse—keeping my hand on her side and watching as Lou's head lolls from side to side. The cantankerous peacock is fast asleep.

Harmony smiles before I open my mouth and removes the scarf from around her head. I'm about to protest when she looks at me with youthful sea-green eyes and tosses my scarf to me.

"I should have done this yesterday," she says, "but having people care for me has been really nice."

Of course she's able to regenerate damaged parts! I should have realized it after witnessing her multiple transformations when we rescued Kumugwe's desiccated body from the island. I'm grateful for one burden removed from my plate and can't imagine having to replace her eyes with some from Kumugwe's vat of snacks.

She slides from Layla's side and lands gracefully on her feet next to me.

"I watched what you did with her army last night. I knew you didn't want to be disturbed. Thank you, Celeste. I'm drained from yesterday's drills, having to constantly restrain the movement of my arms and legs. I'll be happy when you can finally remove this chip."

"Once we stop Lilith and Thurston and their followers, you won't have to worry about the chip anymore," I tell her. "We'll destroy the devices as soon as we disable the people controlling them."

Harmony's beautiful eyes look sad. "I want to see the look in that wicked woman's eyes when she knows she's failed."

The boats are all ashore, and everyone converges around Orville. Chimney runs to me and I brace for his exuberant hug. There's no slowing down with him, and I smile. It's nice to know some things don't change.

"Did you find my sister? And Bridger? And why aren't they with you? Didn't you rescue them? They're okay, right?"

Please-oh-please don't change.

"We'll see them soon, Chim, and yes, they're both doing well. Let's join the others."

Ranger and his mate, Penelope, flank us as we approach the gathering, and I'm humbled by the loyalty of my furry friend. My father sees me from the far side of the group and his worried eyes relax into an expression of gratitude. He smiles. Nick breaks away and walks toward me purposefully, relief and hopefulness in his viridian eyes.

Everyone's here—the animals, the archers, the humans—and Orville motions for me to join him in the center. Before I join him, however, I welcome Nick's gentle embrace.

"We will eat and rest here and listen to what Celeste has learned about those who wish us harm. Sit now, and eat. Celeste?" Orville looks at me to begin, and I walk, holding Nick's hand, to where he stands.

"We're close to the lab," I say. "You made it here faster than I expected, faster than even *you* expected, I think," I hear chuckles in the group, "and my guess is that before the sun reaches its zenith, we'll meet the scientists and their followers here on this beach."

Looking around at all the different expressions I see from fear to excitement, I wait until the murmuring stops.

"We outnumber them already, and they have no powers other than what they'll do out of fear for their leader, Lilith. She's the one to be stopped, but we can't underestimate what her followers will do for their reward. She's protected by some sort of invisible barrier, but with this," I hold Omega high, "she'll fall."

I tell them about the defunct blob army, the training I witnessed with the sinewy humans, and the careless bat creatures.

"What about Blanche," someone asks. "Whose side is she on? And the Overleader—Sharon, I think her name is. What do we do if we see them?"

"Blanche wants to come home," I say, and Chimney's face lights up. "She's afraid of Lilith, though. She's watching over Bridger and Sharon—Sharon isn't a threat anymore. Blanche has been through a lot—we've all been through a lot—and I hope you'll find a way to forgive what she's done."

Some of them nod, others remain undecided.

I tell them more about Sharon's odd condition and how the girl who once terrorized them all as the Overleader is now just an infant. "And I understand some of you with powers

Laurel McHargue

are experiencing fluxes." Many of them nod. "Nevertheless, we *will* prevail over Lilith's army. Every particle of my being is certain of this!" I raise Omega again and look around to see nods and confident smiles.

Orville pats my shoulder, and I nod toward a place outside the group. He follows me.

"We should stay here," I tell him. "Let everyone rest a bit and then dig in. Scatter the boats along the beach with some closer to the foliage so they don't look too suspicious, and then position everyone in places they won't be seen. Lilith's force will come from there," I point eastward down the shoreline toward where I know the lab is, "and she's expecting to march all the way to our village. We'll take them by surprise."

Orville nods slowly. This is not a job he wants, commanding an army of citizens and displaced creatures, but he's the one who should share this plan with them. It's clear the villagers trust him. Regardless of his initial reluctance, he's a natural leader.

"How will they know what to do, and when to do it?" he asks. It's a good question.

"I'll stay unhidden on the beach surrounded by the rest of you in your positions—"

"That is not going to happen," Orville cuts me off and starts to walk away.

"Wait! Hear me out. Lilith will recognize me, and she'll be confused because of how I disappeared from her lab, and I'll have the advantage because I have this," I remind him of my spear. "I'll tell her we have her force surrounded by superior numbers, and she has to surrender or lose them all."

"And when she refuses and sends her people after you?" I knew he'd ask that.

"Then, we all attack with whatever powers and weapons we have. If Nick can stop time just to our front—I don't know if that's possible—we can remove their weapons and,

~ 170 ~

you know, kill them. And if he stops everyone, I'll still be able to disarm them since I'm immune to other people's powers. The bottom line, though, is that with Lilith down, there's no leader."

"What about the bat things?"

"Merts and his archers and you, right? If they come at all, that is. They're lazy and not really loyal to Lilith. They'll be easy to take down.

"How much time till they're in sight?" he asks, and I know he's willing to carry out this plan.

We both squint at the sun, which has risen fully above the horizon.

"I'd say when the sun is there," I point to a place in the sky. "Maybe a bit longer." It's my best guess. "I'm sure Lilith has given up on her blob creatures by now. She'll be angry. That'll be to our advantage too. It'll wear her out."

Orville returns to the gathering to tell them the plan.

I plop down in the sand with Omega on my lap and hope our plan is sound.

~ 35 ~

OMEGA FEELS HEAVY in my lap. Not a good sign.

"Can you penetrate her invisible barrier?" I ask, expecting Omega to glow or shake or turn cold—anything to let me know if I'm preparing to do the right thing—but it remains unchanged.

It doesn't know.

Orville delivers his plan with authority, and as I stand to join the villagers, I see them getting to their feet as well. Their time to rest was brief, but I see in their actions they're ready for this encounter to unfold as it will.

Orville is talking directly to Nick when I arrive.

"Is there any way to test your power before they're here?" he asks.

Nick looks at me before answering, and I sense hesitation. "We'd need people down the beach at different distances for me to try."

"Then we will do this." Orville calls several people by name and tells them the plan.

"Me and Layla'll go too." Lou has woken. He stretches his iridescent head forward from between Layla's ears and spreads out his magnificent tail feathers behind her. A peacock trapped in a metal horse—it's a baffling, beautiful sight. "Just say how far down we gotta go. Don't know about all'a youz, but I'm plumb tuckered. Could use a little down time."

I'm grateful for Lou's ability to make us all chuckle in a time of great uncertainty. Layla walks through the crowd, bows her head low and nudges Orville gently, awaiting instruction.

"I'll place you all and then fly back," he tells our test group. "The rest of you find your places and stay alert. Riku—you, Mac, Celeste, and Ranger, help disperse and conceal our people. Thunder, you and your children will be best hidden in the foliage. Let's go."

With a surge of adrenaline, I feel myself start to glow and come apart.

"Celeste!" Nick's voice snaps me back quickly. He takes my hand and squeezes it. He looks worried. "Help your father hide the kids. They're the least able to defend themselves, and I don't know if I can do this."

He's afraid of trapping himself in time again—he hasn't used his power since his recovery. I hadn't considered that possibility until just now.

"You don't have to do this, Nick," I say, and Riku nods her agreement. "We're well armed and in better physical condition than they are."

"I have to try," he says, but I'm not so sure. What if he does trap himself along with everyone here but me—and Lilith's force shows up? It would be a slaughter.

As if reading my mind, Riku makes the decision.

"No. It is too dangerous. We cannot risk a mistake this close to contact. Nick? You will arm yourself. Mac, you will help the younger adults. And Ranger, you will help our other friends." Her decisive yet gentle way is strangely reassuring. "All should scatter behind Merts and those with weapons, and Celeste, you tell Orville our change of plans."

I feel the burden lift from Nick.

After some initial confusion and much pointing to places from shore to tree line—none of us has done this before—everyone scatters to find concealment, and I meet Orville in the air on his way back.

"That would be disastrous," he agrees. "I'll bring them back, though Lou won't be too happy about the extra effort." He smiles.

"Hey, what was youz thinkin'?" I do a lousy imitation of the snarky peacock and we both laugh, but then a shadow crosses Orville's face.

"Would you . . . could you safely fly east and determine how close they are? I wouldn't ask this if I didn't think you could."

"Of course!" I say. The stress of waiting is exhausting, and I have to put my extra adrenaline to productive use. "I'll know in a jiffy."

And it's good he's sent me on this mission. Lilith and her force will find themselves in our midst before the sun's zenith. From my position in one of the fuller treetops, I see her in the lead, Thurston by her side, and surprisingly, all five bat creatures circling the humans from above. Lilith carries a slim saber, and Thurston, a staff. Walking to the rear of the horde is Blanche, carrying a baby in one arm and holding Bridger's hand with her other.

I expected Blanche would be left behind with the little ones, but I suppose Lilith is confident they'll go on to their next village after conquering ours.

Could I stop her right here, right now? Maybe there doesn't need to be a battle at all! With one throw of my spear, I could take down their leader and shatter their resolve!

"Omega," I whisper, "do I kill Lilith before she reaches our defenses?" *Please-oh-please tell me yes*. The orichalcum in Omega's shaft turns a cold blue and the spear shudders in my hand.

No.

This is troubling. If I can't take her down here, how can I be confident in my ability to stop her when the battle begins? I have to get back to warn them. A flicker of fear sends my blood surging through my veins and I feel like I might explode.

I'm somewhat relieved when I approach our defenses. Other than a few empty or upturned boats here and there, I see no indication of a living presence. Everyone is well hidden, even Thunder, who must be crouching in the underbrush with his multicolored cubs. I'm sure he's camouflaged Eenie and her kittens far behind him.

Orville appears from behind a sandy dune and waves me to him, and I tell him what I know. He takes me to each defensive position—behind trees, in foliage, under some of the upturned boats, dug in behind dunes and in hasty trenches—and we share words of encouragement with every member of the village before returning to his place behind the dune, where Riku and several others are dug in and out of sight.

We don't have to wait long.

"What are these?" Lilith's screeching voice shatters the unnatural silence surrounding us. Even the water seems fearful of splashing onto the shore. "Boats? Find the people!"

I can't let them get to the boats, under which several frightened villagers hide waiting for a signal to attack, and suddenly, everything happens too quickly.

I leap to the top of the dune. "You're surrounded, Lilith!" I scream, holding Omega high. Throw down your weapons and surrender!"

"Deceiver!" she yells, pointing her saber at me, and then she laughs hideously. "Get the girl, batkins! Destroy her!"

"Fire!" I shout, and arrows whizz through the air, taking down three of the bats, but two are nearly on top of me. I leap into the air holding Omega above me with both hands and plunge it into the closest bat, which releases a grotesque grunt before falling to the ground. Orville attacks the other—they grapple in the air and I fear for my friend—as I land and pull my spear from the repugnant creature's belly, my first kill, and all around me is chaos.

Lilith's humans battle with ours, whose weapons are better than theirs, though our close-in fighting has never been tested, and I see our children start to appear—they stand still in their places, like innocent statues, and the horde becomes distracted by them, they don't know what to do, and here and there I see a person freeze in place—Katie's power! She's freezing them all, one by one!—and I hear them shatter and see them fall when our villagers strike, and when Thunder and Ranger and Layla burst from their places, Lilith starts her retreat with Thurston and I have to kill her, I have to kill her, and I hurl Omega with all my strength and my aim is true but when it reaches Lilith it bounces back and returns to my hands—DAMN IT!—and I hear her cackle again and then I see Bridger break from Blanche's side and run past Lilith who tries to grab him but he's too fast, he's running toward me, toward me, but I'm too far away and before I can reach him, Chimney rushes out to rescue him and then . . . and then—

"You'll not work for them, builder!" Lilith screeches and hurls her saber at little Bridger—he's just a boy!—but Chimney's already between him and Lilith, his back to the impending projectile, his arms reaching for his friend . . . and then no! No! NO! My beautiful young buddy stumbles, his eyes grow wide, he's still reaching . . . reaching . . . there's pain in his eyes . . . and he stumbles and stumbles and falls—he falls at the feet of the boy who builds things—

"NO!" My voice joins with Blanche's and others across the blood-splattered beach and the surf suddenly rises and crashes with our screams and Blanche runs to her brother—

"NO!" Thurston's voice booms over the wailing and there's no one on their side left to fight and we all watch as he drops his staff and lifts his wife from the ground—she kicks and punches at him and struggles to free herself—but he stands tall, he stands tall like a man, and yes! Yes! He reconnects to a glimmer of humanity deep inside him—I feel it! I feel his sorrow, feel his regret!—and he marches purposefully with Lilith writhing in his grasp past Harmony into the pounding surf—

"NO!" Lilith screeches for the last time before they're both submerged and her hideous voice is swallowed by the sea—

Ah!

Harmony stands in the water at the edge of the shoreline and turns back to me and smiles—

Orville—his right wing torn away from his shoulder from battling with a bat-creature—limps toward the circle forming around Bridger, the baby, and Blanche, who cradles her brother in her lap.

"No, Chim, no! Don't disappear on me now! I'm back! I'll never leave you again, I promise, I'm sorry! I'm so, so sorry! Help! Someone please help! I should have taken you with me! NO! I should have stayed!"

Blanche's tears soak Chimney's cheeks as she rocks him like a baby. "We'll go home now, and you can rest, and I'll be nicer to you, I'll be nicer to everyone, I promise I will! And I won't be such a boss, and I'll—"

"It's okay, Blanche. I love you too," he whispers, and Ryder pushes his way through the solemn crowd—Yes! He'll save our sweet, gifted snoodle gatherer!

But no.

No. He's too late.

For the last time, Chimney Maxibillion McDade fades from sight. Not even I can see him.

~ 36 ~

"WHERE IS HE? Where is he, Celeste? You can see him, I know you can! Chim? Wake up, Chim! Tell me he's here, Celeste, right here in my lap, and we'll take him home now!" Blanche looks up at me with tragic eyes blurred with tears. Her hands search for a boy who's no longer here.

I sit by her side and wrap my arms around her. She leans into me and sobs, and I cry with her. We all cry with her. Time feels suspended and everything feels unreal. Nick drops to his knees behind us, encircling us both in his arms for minutes or hours until there are no more tears.

The sea is calm again, Harmony remains at its edge, gazing out over its gentle swells—vigilant—and the infant Sharon cries.

Nick helps me to my feet, and I offer Blanche my hand. After one last futile search for her brother, she takes my hand and stands.

"Let's go home, Blanche," I say. "Lilith is gone. It's over."

She takes Sharon from Bridger, whose tears have washed streaks of grime from his little face, and rocks the baby gently until she's quiet.

Looking around at this circle of friends, I see sorrow, exhaustion, injury, and pain, but no fear. Chimney was our one loss, our most heartbreaking loss.

Ryder will have much to do to heal our injured, if his powers remain steady.

Our enemies lie shattered in frozen fragments across the sand like pieces of some morbid puzzle, and Harmony walks back to us slowly. She looks over her shoulder once, but no one follows her from the sea.

"I'm going home," she tells us all. "Goodbye, baby sister." She strokes Sharon's wet cheek and without waiting for a response, turns and runs back to the water, back to what she knows. And when she leaps from sand to sea in a graceful dive, we gasp as her glimmering, opalescent tail appears before vanishing beneath the surface.

We stand, quietly watching, until we know she too will not return from the sea.

And then, without another word, we leave the boats and walk together, as one, toward the setting sun, toward home.

~ ~ ~ ~ ~

Just before we reach the village, our silent trudge is halted by the raucous caw of two huge ravens circling above. Huginn and Muninn. Why are they here? We find our answer as soon as we see the houses.

"Welcome home, Celeste!" Odin's voice carries across the space between us. He squints his one eye at me and stands from where he's been sitting on the porch steps. His wolves sit by his side. He appears as he did when I first saw him in the sandcastle a lifetime ago, when I thought I was home, and he delivered a package as George, the ham man—his cloak, his floppy hat, his eye patch, all unchanged.

Ranger and Penelope and Thunder surround me in an instant, their guttural growls warning the wolves they'd better stay where they stand.

"I won't go back with you!" I shout.

"I am not here to take you away, girl. Come. Come, all of you. We are here in peace." Huginn and Muninn settle on a rooftop, and his wolves recline at his feet, their backs toward us.

We all walk toward him together.

"Do you trust him, Celeste?" Nick whispers in my ear.

"No. But I'm not afraid of him anymore."

"Odin! Why are you here?" Orville strides forward commandingly and stands in front of the ancient god. I wince when I see my friend's severed wing.

Odin waits until we're all in close before answering. "I am old. I am tired. But most of all, I am lonely."

The villagers mumble and he waits for them to stop.

"When Celeste was by my side, I found new hope that I could survive and be happy. But she did not belong forever in Oblivia."

He pauses, studying me intensely with his eye, and smiles when Dad rushes to my side and wraps an arm around me. The two men stare at one another for a while before Odin speaks again.

"And so, I come to you," he points to his wolves and ravens, "we come to you—with one request. Simply put, we ask to live out our lives here, with you, on this planet, as mortals."

Orville and Nick look to me, their eyebrows raised in astonishment. It's not lost on any of us that this was a suggestion Chimney had made not long ago. We had laughed, then.

"But, the rain!" Blanche speaks up, and I take it as a good sign. She's thinking about her community, thinking about life.

"The rain will come, the rain will go, it will happen as it has without my meddling. There are forces far greater even than mine at work in this universe."

"If we let you stay, will you protect us against other threats to our safety?" Mac asks.

"I will take up arms as you have, if necessary, and fight as a man."

He would sacrifice his powers to live with us—and someday, to die.

Orville turns to face us. "Are there any objections to Odin's request? Is there need for further discussion?"

The villagers are stunned to silence.

I study Odin's wizened face and try to imagine him as just a man. Then I remember the times I've been called just a girl, and more than just a girl. Who's to decide what drives us to be who we are, and more than who we are? And how long will a centuries-old god live once he abandons his realm?

Orville waits for someone to speak, and from the crowd, Blanche walks forward, passes Orville, and hands the infant to Odin. He holds her gently in his crooked hands, and a tear falls from his eye.

~ ~ ~ ~ ~

The night is filled with sounds of soft conversation, weeping, chuckling, and sighing. I rest in Nick's arms in the field beyond Teresa's garden and we watch as stars grow brighter and comets streak across the sky.

"It's over, right?" he whispers. "And you're back." His fingers caress my cheeks, the outline of my lips, my neck. "I love you, Pipsqueak."

I tremble and tingle. I can't speak. He doesn't wait for my answer, though, and when he presses his lips to mine, when he holds me more tightly in his own trembling arms, I lose myself in him—my particles releasing themselves to join with his in a way that frightens me, in a way that frightens him—and when he tries to release me, to end his glorious kiss, we both feel a pain that feels like death.

I can't do this to him anymore. I can't keep hurting him.

I pull away from him and stand, my body still glowing and nebulous, and I struggle to pull myself together.

"I love you too, Nick!" I say. "Tell my father I'm sorry! Tell him . . . we'll find each other again in another time!"

And then I turn and run and fly toward the sea.

~ 37 ~

I AM MORE than Celeste Araia Nolan, though I didn't ask to be. With Omega in hand, I fly through darkness over the turbulent water until a familiar precipice rises from the horizon. I will see Old Man Massive once more before I leave.

"Little Paloma," his whisper booms, "you have come to say goodbye. Thank you, child."

To an old mountain spirit, everyone is a child.

I stand on his bulbous nose, the same place I've stood time and time before, but I'm not the same girl.

"How do you know, Old Man?" How has he known to do or say any of the things he's done for me and said since I ran away from the children's home?

"I do not know how. I simply know what I feel."

"Is this the right choice, though?" Even before he answers, Omega glows warmly in my hand.

"Unlike me, you were never meant to stay. I felt this from the moment you woke me, though it saddens me."

"You saved my life more than once, and my friends' lives. Thank you, Old Man. I won't be burdening you again."

"You never have burdened me, little dove. You have given me a purpose for the brief times your path has touched mine. A greater purpose awaits you."

"How can that be? Haven't I done enough already?" I feel a tantrum coming on.

"Almost, child. You have made a decision. Follow it, and you will see."

His words fill me with a sense of serenity unlike I've ever felt before.

"There *is* one more thing I know I have to do," I say, and I lay Omega in the crease of his nose, in a place I once rested myself.

The mark on the back of my head tingles and I let myself disperse in the air above my mountain friend. I spread myself thin like a blanket, and then drop myself down upon his craggy boulders in a warm embrace.

This is how I hug a mountain.

He chuckles. It starts slowly, and my particles jiggle until he laughs with abandon and I'm bounced back into the air. When he stops laughing, I snap back into myself and recover my spear.

"What a gift you are, child. Now go. Remember me in your dreams."

He closes his eye and I lift from his nose, leaving an amused grin on his bearded profile. Just as I start skyward, however, flames shoot through the darkness and Noor sweeps beneath me, tumbling me onto her back.

"Don't you dare!" I shout at her. "I'm finished with the gods!" Even if she tries to drop me back into the sea, I'll dissipate and she'll never find me.

"Settle yourself, Celeste. I am here to help you find your way." Noor's voice is hypnotic, and although I have no reason to trust her—why didn't she come when I called for help in the past?—I feel I'm where I should be.

I say nothing, but cling to her back as the wind whips past. She's taking me to the other side again, but I don't want to go there. I can't return.

"Only for a moment," she says, reading my mind.

And then I see she's not taking me to the village, she's taking me to the abandoned lab. Before I can ask why, Noor unleashes a stunning blast of flames and the building explodes into ashes. Lilith's mangled army bubbles and bursts into a choking sulfurous gas, and the gigantic dragonfly lifts up and away in a breathtaking arc.

As I ride her into the heavens, I'm reminded of an image at the top of the great door to Odin's dining hall. It appeared to be a figure riding a fire-breathing winged creature.

I shiver as the air grows thin and my flimsy dress flutters around me. We pass through the nacreous clouds of the realm once belonging to the god who only wanted someone to grow old with, and we keep climbing until I feel I'll float away.

"This is where I leave you, Celeste. This is where your burdens end."

"But wait!" I call to Noor as she drops from sight.

I'm left alone in the universe, floating among countless galaxies with nothing but Omega, my dress, and my emerald scarf.

I can't return to my father and the place that felt like home with my new friends. Old Man Massive knows this. Whatever I am, I'm too dangerous to be close to those I love.

The spear is no use to me here—and Omega should never again fall into the hands of people who could use it for evil, people on the planet even now with anger in their hearts and cruel, selfish desires.

I know what I have to do.

I look toward the planet where good people will mourn my disappearance, and my last teardrops as a girl breach the brims of my eyes. The choice is mine: wipe them away or let them fall. I let them run down my cheeks and drop through the atmosphere.

My teardrops undulate and grow in size as they plunge toward the planet, and I know what will happen when they reach the troubled orb.

I unzip my dress and slip it from me, releasing it to the universe. I won't be snapping back into it ever again. I pull my curls free from my silk scarf—stained with my blood and Nick's and Harmony's—and push it away to follow my teardrops.

And I am free.

"Never to return!" I shout, and just as I once threw this spear into the sea, I hurl Omega into the heavens far, far away from a planet I once called home.

Never is forever now.

Omega bursts into flames before it's out of sight, and a thrill shivers my body because I feel in my slowly dissipating particles that its destruction ends the powers and fluxes that have plagued and perplexed those on the planet below.

They will learn to thrive in a natural world on a planet soon to be reborn.

I dissolve into the universe, into my final form, and I smell honey-lemon muffins! My mother is here! Zoya is too, floating among the galaxies with her children. And I feel Chimney's presence.

I'm here, Chim! Don't be afraid!

I tell him we have not died, we'll never die, we're here—home!—with all who arrived before us.

My particles disperse until they're everywhere and nowhere, and I feel euphoric. My teardrops are about to splash into the sea of the living planet, and when they do, they'll cause a flood that will engulf it all.

It's happening, and my molecules feel the fear and chaos of those submerged.

Breathe! I tell them all—all across the planet—because I'm everywhere now and a part of me is in each of them. *Remember you can breathe!*

And I feel a rebalancing across the planet as the waters recede. Those with goodness in their hearts discover they can live both submerged and topside, and those with wicked intentions will feed Kumugwe's realm.

Nick emerges from the water believing he'll never love anyone the way he loves me, and he won't, but I see her emerge—the girl who will find my scarf washed up on a beach after the flood—and when she finds Nick, he'll recognize it and know she's the one he will be with. He'll see me in her eyes because I'll be there. I'll be a part of everything and everyone.

And I see other things—things that have yet to happen.

After years of helping my father and Blanche raise baby Sharon in a nurturing, healthy home, Odin will transform and share in the wonders I'm discovering here—wonders greater than those he enjoyed as a god. He will not regret the decision he made to become human before his transformation.

My loyal animal friends will propagate and live in harmony with humans until they transform, and then they too will join me in this unencumbered state.

Katie, Lena, Jack, Bridger, Ryder, and Maddie will find partners to grow old with until their final transformation, and their healthy, copper-skinned babies will frolic on land and in the sea. Some will return from their day's adventures with stories of a beautiful opalescent mermaid who sings to them, and an underwater castle held up by sea lions, and vats filled with eyeballs.

Merts will emerge from the water as they were before The Event, as three—father, mother, and child—and Layla will shake her shining copper-color coat of hair, releasing Lou from his bondage, though he will ride with her upon her back until their time on the planet is over.

A wingless Orville and Riku will soon add twin babies—Charlie and Claire—to the village, and baby Aiden will be born to Mac and Teresa shortly thereafter. They will become the new leaders of their village and beyond, and they will lead with fairness and with pure intentions in their hearts.

And they will enthrall others across the planet with the stories Orville has shared with them . . . stories of a girl he once met in a dream, a girl he rescued and who rescued him, a girl with powers no human should ever possess, a girl named Celeste Araia Nolan.

And those who listen will meet me in their dreams.

~ Acknowledgments ~

Mike McHargue, husband of mine for over 35 adventure-filled years, thank you for being the greatest patron of my work. I would not have been able to complete and publish the number of books I have out there in the world without your constant encouragement and belief that what I'm creating is far better than good.

Carol Bellhouse, thank you for your timely, spot-on, and intuitive chapter-by-chapter edits of this last *Waterwight* book. Your bubble bath recordings kept me focused, motivated, and amused. Someday I may share them with the world.

Stephanie Spong, thank you for staying up all night to read and reread this book so you could provide me with (pages and pages of) insightful advice for making Celeste's final adventure memorable in a big way. I have a sack of potatoes waiting for you at my house.

John Orville Stewart, namesake for one of my most significant characters, thank you for continuing to inspire new ideas during our morning walks.

Cindy Jewkes of *Good Tales Editing*, thank you for proofreading my final manuscript. More books from me await your eagle eyes.

Thanks to my beta readers Judy Cole and Kelly Burggraaf for your suggestions on how to improve different elements of this book.

Ashley Larson, thank you for working the kinks from my writing muscles. You are a massage therapist extraordinaire.

Thanks to my 2018-2019 Patreon patrons of my podcast ***Alligator Preserves*** for supporting my creativity on air and helping to provide needed funding for the production costs of this book: Susan B. Russo, Charlene McDade, Carol Shaughnessy, Stephanie Spong, Donna Baier Stein, Erin Sue Grantham, Mimi Finch, Mary Jelf, Jake McHargue, Mary Wilson, Brenda Sebern, and Sean Toodle. ;)

Thanks also to Leadville locals who continue to support my writing with their services and promotion: Beth and Kenny Donoher at *Silver City Printing*, Brenda Marine at *B&B Shipping and More*, Elise Sunday at *Fire On The Mountain*, and Marcia Martinek at the *Herald Democrat*.

Thank you, Mum and Dad (may you both exist in peace in places far away and very near) for tolerating years of my dream sharing. Who knew, way back then, what inspiration they would bring to my writing?

Thank you, Marilyn Hintsa, my best buddy since kindergarten. You knew my dreams would become books!

And of course, thank you, kind readers. If you enjoyed this final adventure with Celeste and the characters who shared her quest, please consider recommending the series to a friend and posting a review on Amazon!

~ About the Author ~

LAUREL McHARGUE was raised in Braintree, Massachusetts, but somehow found her way to the breathtaking mountains of Colorado, where she has taught and currently lives with her husband and Ranger, the German Shepherd.

She dreams in Technicolor, writes in many genres, and hosts the podcast *Alligator Preserves*. Check out Laurel's blog, where she writes about life—real and imagined.

www.leadvillelaurel.com

~ A Personal Note from Laurel ~

I would love to hear from you!
Connect with me here:

Facebook: Leadville Laurel (author page)
Twitter: @LeadvilleLaurel
LinkedIn: Laurel (Bernier) McHargue
Web Page: www.leadvillelaurel.com
Email: laurel@strackpress.com
Podcast: Alligator Preserves

Check out my other books on my Amazon Author page
and let me know what you think!

And remember, we struggling authors/musicians/artists/actors
love positive feedback, so if you like what we do, please
consider writing reviews of our work! If you don't like what
we do, well, if you can't say something nice . . .

SYNONYM GLOSSARY

Aberrant	Abnormal, unusual, deviant
Abominable	Awful, horrible, monstrous
Abomination	Horror, eyesore, disgrace
Abrupt	Sudden, unexpected, quick
Adversary	Opponent, rival, enemy
Alabaster	Soft white, semi-translucent
Amnesia	Loss of memory
Aninnik	Inuit word for breath
Ashen	Pale, pasty, gray
Balk	Resist, refuse, thwart
Beckon	Summon, signal, motion
Betray	Deceive, bluff, trick
Bolster	Boost, strengthen, encourage
Breach	Open, break, crack
Bulbous	Round, bulging, swollen
Cantankerous	Irritable, crabby, argumentative
Careening	Speeding, traversing, traveling
Censure	Criticism, disapproval, scorn
Chastise	Reprimand, scold, rebuke
Chimera	Fantasy, illusion, figment
Churning	Rolling, mixing, agitating

SYNONYM GLOSSARY

Claustrophobia	Fear of enclosed spaces
Competence	Ability, skill, fitness
Consequence	Significance, penalty, cost
Constrict	Tighten, narrow, squeeze
Convoluted	Complicated, difficult, intricate
Culprit	Offender, criminal, wrongdoer
Defunct	Obsolete, outdated, useless
Demeanor	Manner, conduct, behavior
Demise	Death, end, expiration
Desiccated	Dried, shriveled, shrunken
Devastated	Upset, overwhelmed, shattered
Dilate	Open, widen, expand`
Discombobulated	Confused, shaken, upset
Disheveled	Ruffled, untidy, scruffy
Dissipating	Dispersing, dissolving, scattering
Distended	Swollen, bloated, inflated
Dumbfounded	Surprised, amazed, stunned
Enthrall	Captivate, charm, fascinate
Enthusiastic	Excited, eager, passionate
Entourage	Backup, support, following
Eons	Ages, eternity, forever

SYNONYM GLOSSARY

Euphoria	Elation, joy, bliss
Evasion	Avoidance, dodging, fudging
Exacerbated	Worsened, intensified, aggravated
Excruciating	Agonizing, unbearable, painful
Feigned	Pretend, contrived, artificial
Fervent	Passionate, eager, enthusiastic
Filament	Thread, strand, string
Fissure	Crack, gap, opening
Furrow	Crease, wrinkle, pucker
Ghastly	Grim, horrific, shocking
Havoc	Chaos, destruction, devastation
Heinous	Monstrous, terrible, dreadful
Horde	Pack, group, gang
Immune	Resistant, protected, invulnerable
Impending	Looming, approaching, coming
Implore	Beg, plead, appeal
Inanely	Ridiculously, childishly, mindlessly
Incapacitate	Harm, disable, weaken
Incessant	Ceaseless, relentless, persistent
Infiltrate	Penetrate, permeate, intrude
Ingenious	Clever, inventive, imaginative

SYNONYM GLOSSARY

Intentions	Aims, goals, objectives
Interloper	Intruder, snoop, imposter
Invigorating	Stimulating, refreshing, brisk
Invocation	Call, request, appeal
Lilting	Sweet, pleasing, melodious
Ludicrous	Absurd, ridiculous, nonsensical
Lull	Quiet, calm, stillness
Malevolent	Wicked, vindictive, unkind
Manipulate	Operate, use, control
Meager	Skimpy, inadequate, measly
Meandering	Twisting, winding, bending
Mesmerize	Hypnotize, captivate, enthrall
Mirage	Vision, illusion, hallucination
Mirthless	Cheerless, dreary, humorless
Miscreant	Troublemaker, villain, criminal
Myriad	Countless, innumerable, many
Nacreous	Lustrous, shimmering, polychromatic
Oblivious	Unaware, ignorant, insensible
Omniscient	All-knowing, all-seeing, wise
Opalescent	Bright, iridescent, polychromatic
Optimism	Hopefulness, confidence, positivity

SYNONYM GLOSSARY

Permeate	Flood, fill, soak
Perplexed	Baffled, confused, mystified
Petulant	Sulky, grumpy, moody
Plagued	Afflicted, tortured, troubled
Plaintive	Sad, mournful, sorrowful
Posse	Gang, group, crew
Predicament	Difficulty, dilemma, quandary
Predict	Foresee, guess, expect
Pristine	Perfect, untouched, unspoiled
Prominent	Noticeable, conspicuous, projecting
Pungent	Overpowering, sharp, bitter
Puny	Weak, tiny, feeble
Realm	Kingdom, domain, territory
Regress	Go back, retreat, revert
Reluctant	Unwilling, hesitant, averse
Remnants	Traces, pieces, scraps
Repugnant	Offensive, distasteful, obnoxious
Resolve	Determination, resolution, tenacity
Reverberate	Echo, resound, vibrate
Reverie	Daydream, contemplation, musing
Rivulet	Trickle, stream, creek

SYNONYM GLOSSARY

Searing	Shooting, burning, stabbing
Serenity	Calmness, peacefulness, stillness
Sinewy	Lean, wiry, strong
Smug	Self-satisfied, superior, haughty
Sneer	Scorn, snicker, jeer
Solemnity	Seriousness, somberness, gravity
Sonorous	Echoing, resonant, deep
Striated	Streaked, banded, striped
Subdue	Conquer, defeat, vanquish
Subjugate	Subdue, defeat, suppress
Summon	Call, bid, beckon
Surreptitious	Secret, sneaky, furtive
Tentative	Hesitant, uncertain, timid
Thrive	Succeed, prosper, flourish
Torturous	Agonizing, excruciating, punishing
Trudge	Walk heavily, stumble, plod
Tsunami	Tidal wave
Turbulent	Choppy, wavy, tempestuous
Turmoil	Chaos, disorder, confusion
Undulation	Wave, ripple, flutter
Unencumbered	Free as a bird

SYNONYM GLOSSARY

Unwavering	Solid, steadfast, resolute
Utterance	Sound, exclamation, statement
Vague	Unclear, nebulous, ambiguous
Vanquish	Crush, defeat, conquer
Verbose	Talkative, wordy, rambling
Vigilant	Watchful, alert, cautious
Vulnerable	Weak, helpless, exposed
Wary	Cautious, guarded, suspicious
Wince	Cringe, shudder, flinch
Wizened	Wrinkled, lined, aged
Zenith	Peak, summit, highpoint

QUESTIONS FOR DISCUSSION

1. In what ways does Book III differ from I and II?

2. What new challenges does Celeste encounter?

3. How does Celeste's relationship with the gods change?

4. How do the gods change in this last book?

5. What is the significance of the following:
   a. Vision/eyes
   b. Fathers
   c. Fluxes
   d. Celeste's scarf
   e. Home
   f. Tears
   g. The Spear
   h. Time
   i. Darkness
   j. Rebirth

6. How does Blanche change?

7. What will happen to Sharon?

8. Who/what is Noor?

9. How has Celeste grown in this book?

10. Why does Celeste make her final decision?